HOT FUDGE HOMICIDE

A SEASIDE ICE CREAM SHOP MYSTERY (BOOK 4)

ANGELA K. RYAN

JOHN PAUL PUBLISHING

CHAPTER 1

*A*nna glanced at the strawberry ice cream cone clock on the wall.

It was 12:15, which meant that Jack was already fifteen minutes late. This was not like Anna's sixteen-year-old employee. Jack had proven himself to be a responsible teenager over the four months since Anna opened her ice cream shop, *Bella's Dream,* in the coastal Massachusetts town of Seagull Cove.

As much as Anna tried to push it aside, a feeling that something wasn't right settled into her chest.

Anna's cell phone vibrated in her pocket. She pulled it out with lighting speed. Jack's name had popped onto her screen.

"Hey, Jack. Where are you? Is everything okay?"

"I'm so sorry, Anna, but I woke up with a bad case of the flu this morning. I planned to call, but I fell back asleep and just woke up. I'm not going to be able to help you with the hot fudge sundae bar at that party this afternoon. I would try to find a replacement, but I think I'm too sick to even do that, and it's probably too late, anyway. I'm so sorry for the last-minute notice."

"I'm sorry to hear that, Jack. I hope you feel..." Anna started to say before Jack cut her off.

"I have to go. Right now!"

Anna was about to say, "Feel better soon," but Jack disconnected the call before she could get the words out.

She tried not to panic. She could do this alone if she absolutely *had* to.

At least she hoped she could. It was her first hot fudge sundae bar, and she really could use an extra set of hands.

"Hey, Anna, you look as white as a ghost. Are you okay?" She hadn't noticed Kathy, one of her staff members, standing a short distance away. A recently retired executive assistant, Kathy was good at thinking under pressure. Maybe she could help.

"Remember that anniversary party this afternoon?"

"The one celebrating Allie and Jackson's first anniversary? Aren't you hosting a hot-fudge sundae bar at that party?" Allie and Jackson were regulars at *Bella's Dream*, so most of the staff knew them.

"Yes. I'm supposed to be set up and ready to go by 2:00. Jack was supposed to help me, but he just called to tell me that he has a bad case of the flu."

"Yikes. Do you want me to help you, instead?"

Anna looked at her other two employees. Ethan and Sarah were both in high school, and Anna liked to have three employees in the shop, including one adult, on weekends. And it was shaping up to be a sunny day. The busy summer season was over, so she dropped down to two employees on weekdays, but weekends could still get busy. People came from far and wide to enjoy the New England fall foliage. "I don't think so, Kathy. I need you here. It's a beautiful October Saturday, and it's bound to get busy."

"It will be hard to find a replacement for Jack on such short notice. Too bad Velma's at a wedding. Can you manage the sundae bar by yourself?" Kathy asked.

"I suppose I'll have to. But it's my first one, so I thought it would go more smoothly with two people. Besides, there's a lot of stuff to lug in and out of Allie's and Jackson's house."

"I can help," came a voice from across the counter.

Anna turned around to find Todd Devonshire, one of her regular customers, grinning in her direction.

"I couldn't help but overhear. I just finished meeting with a client, and I have the rest of the afternoon free. I'd be happy to lend a hand." Todd was a financial planner who lived in nearby Gloucester. He had several clients in Seagull Cove, and whenever he came to town for a meeting, he would make it a point to stop in *Bella's Dream* for an ice cream. Velma thought it had more to do with his interest in Anna than in ice cream. Todd was cute. And charming. But Anna had more than enough to do with a new business and her search for her sister. Investing in a new relationship wasn't likely to happen anytime soon.

"I can't ask you to give up a Saturday afternoon to help me run a hot fudge sundae bar." But even as she spoke those words, Anna had a feeling she was going to ask, anyway. Fortunately, Todd made it easy.

"You *didn't* ask. I offered. Besides, it's not like I'm doing it for free. I will expect payment in the form of a hot fudge sundae," he said with a wink.

"I would be forever grateful," Anna said in relief.

"It's my pleasure. Just tell me what to do."

Anna led Todd into the supply room, where the previous evening she had filled plastic boxes with jars of toppings and paper goods in order to save time today.

"You can start by helping me load these supplies into my car," Anna said. "Allie and Jackson have a second freezer in their basement, so I brought the ice cream over last night."

Anna and Todd each grabbed two boxes and brought them to the alley out back, where Anna had parked her car.

"This one smells delicious," Todd said, pulling the box to his nose and breathing in the sweet scents.

"You've got one of the boxes with the dry toppings. I got off easy with the paper goods," Anna chuckled.

Anna filled one more box with items from the refrigerator, then they piled the rest of the boxes into Anna's backseat and trunk and drove across town to Jackson's and Allie's home. Anna glanced at the clock on her dashboard. "We're just on time. Guests should be in the middle of lunch now, so that will give us enough time to set up before they are ready for dessert. I can't thank you enough, Todd. Without your help, I would have been late."

"Don't mention it. This was a fun change to my afternoon plans. I'm glad to see you're branching out and getting creative with business opportunities. Hosting sundae bars at events like this is a great idea to expand your business now that the summer foot traffic has died down on Main Street."

"It came about spontaneously. Jackson and Allie, the guests of honor, were in my shop a couple of weeks ago talking about their first anniversary party. So, I pitched the idea of a hot fudge sundae bar, and they loved it. I've never done it before, but what could possibly go wrong?"

"Hopefully, satisfied guests will spread the word, and more opportunities will come your way."

"That's what I'm counting on," Anna said, patting her pocket. "Jackson and Allie agreed to let me put out some business cards, so I brought plenty."

They unloaded the car and hauled the boxes into the living room, which was strangely somber for an anniversary celebration. It was a small house with an open concept living room and dining room, so guests were mostly scattered about between those two rooms.

Todd looked at the quiet crowd and gave Anna a confused look.

She shrugged her shoulders.

"Excuse me, Uncle Chester," Allie said, practically leaping up to greet Anna and Todd. "Boy, am I glad to see you," she said softly. "This party is dull. Jackson was right. We should have had a separate gathering for our friends and family, but I thought it would be a good chance to bring everyone together. My family is bringing this party down big time."

"Maybe the ice cream sundaes will liven things up," Todd said.

"Allie, this is Todd Devonshire. He's my assistant for the day," Anna said.

"The guests are just finishing lunch, so we'll be ready for you soon. You can start setting up now," Allie said, looking over at Jackson, who was talking to an older woman and sending her a look that seemed to plead, 'help me.' Allie directed Anna to a long folding table covered by a plastic red and white checkered tablecloth. "You can set up here. I'd better go. Aunt Violet cornered Jackson ten minutes ago, and she hasn't come up for air since."

"Leave everything to us," Anna said. "We'll be ready for customers in no time."

Allie turned to head toward Jackson, but the man whom she had addressed earlier as 'Uncle Chester' waved her over to where he was sitting. "Allie, please come over here and tell me where you ordered this food from. You should really ask for a refund. The chicken is dry, and the vegetables are soggy."

Violet, the woman Jackson had been talking to, rushed to Chester's side.

Allie rolled her eyes at Anna and Todd. "Uncle Chester is being his usual difficult self. If you need anything, let me know. And if you get thirsty, drinks are in the kitchen."

"Good luck," Anna mouthed.

"Put me to work," Todd said. "What can I do?"

"How about if you unload the boxes from the car, and I'll start setting up the table?"

"Works for me. You can be the brains of the operation, and I'll be the brawn."

Anna set glass serving bowls and decorative spoons onto the table and began filling them with colorful, sweet-smelling toppings. Then she went to the kitchen to warm up the hot fudge and caramel and sent Todd to the freezer in the basement for the tubs of ice cream she had brought the night before.

After she had transformed the folding table into a hot fudge sundae bar, Anna stepped back to admire the spread. It was a colorful smorgasbord of toppings, including hot fudge, caramel, syrupy strawberries, nuts, cherries, jimmies, multicolored sprinkles, chocolate chips, coconut flakes, crushed cookies, peanut butter cups, crushed Heath bars, whipped cream, and marshmallows.

"It looks delicious, if I do say so myself," Anna said.

"I want to eat it all," Todd said.

"How about if you scoop the chocolate, and I'll scoop the vanilla? The guests can help themselves to the toppings."

"Of course. That's half the fun."

Allie and Jackson invited their guests to the sundae bar, which seemed to inject a bit of energy into the previously lifeless crowd.

The couple stood next to Anna and Todd, greeting their guests as they approached the table.

Anna glanced at the front door and had to laugh. "What is Casper doing here?"

Allie rolled her eyes. "Someone let him in earlier, and I didn't have the heart to throw him out. But I think he's ready to leave, now that lunch is over. I'll let him out."

Chester was the first one at the hot fudge sundae bar, with Violet next to him.

"What a great idea, Allie!" Violet said, her eyes wide open as Anna handed her a bowl of vanilla ice cream.

She made her way through the bar, piling a little of everything into her bowl. "More scooping and less talking, Violet. You're standing in front of the sprinkles," Chester said.

"Give Aunt Violet a break," a tall man wearing round eyeglasses and a tweed jacket said.

"That's my cousin, Drake," Allie whispered to Anna.

"Don't worry," Anna assured the guests. "We brought plenty of everything. Here, I'll just make a second dish of sprinkles and put it on the other side of the table."

"Don't mind Uncle Chester," Drake said under his breath. "He's in quite the mood today."

Jackson nodded. "We noticed."

Drake leaned toward to the man standing next him. "Your brother is a piece of work, Dad."

"Always has been, always will be," the man said, glaring at his brother and not bothering to whisper.

"What's that, Nicholas?" Chester asked.

"Nothing, Chester. I was talking to Drake."

"Quiet, Uncle Nick," Allie said, putting her finger to her lips. "If he hears you, you'll put him in an even *worse* mood."

Nick shook his head. "I'll never understand why my brother insists on calling me Nicholas. I've gone by Nick since high school."

"Probably because he knows you prefer Nick," Drake said. "Uncle Chester's grumpiness has been getting worse. I don't know how Aunt Violet puts up with him."

Nick looked thoughtfully at Chester and Violet. "She seems to have more patience with him now than ever before. I don't know how she does it. Or why, for that matter."

As the guests made their way through the line and began enjoying their sundaes, the mood of the party seemed to lift. Once they settled down with their ice creams, chatter filled the room.

Allie and Jackson noticed, too.

"It's the magic of ice cream," Anna said with a satisfied smile.

Before the last guest had gone through the line, Chester stood up, wearing a sour expression, and made a beeline to the sundae bar.

"Oh, great," Allie said under her breath. "What now?"

"My hot fudge tastes funny," Chester said, holding his face a few inches from Anna's. Then he turned to face the others. "Does anyone else's hot fudge taste strange?"

"Oh, quiet down," a woman said. "First, you complained about the food, which was absolutely delicious, by the way. Now you're complaining about the hot fudge."

"Don't tell me to be quiet, Dorothea. I'm telling you, the hot fudge doesn't taste right. Don't you pay for this, Jackson. Do you hear me?"

Anna took a clean plastic spoon and tasted the fudge from one of the glass bowls. It was perfect. "It tastes fine to me," Anna said to Allie.

Todd did the same thing. "It's wonderful. I can't imagine what he's complaining about."

Anna offered Chester another sundae with a different topping. "We also have caramel and strawberries, if you're not a fan of the fudge."

"Maybe I will," Chester said.

Anna gave him another scoop of vanilla, and this time he filled his dish with warm caramel and an array of toppings.

"Much better," he said.

"Don't mind Chester," a woman wearing grey dress slacks and a navy cardigan said. "I've worked for that man for fifteen years, and he's never satisfied with anything. The fudge is heavenly."

Anna smiled. "Thank you."

The woman grabbed one of Anna's business cards. "My name is Eliza. I may be interested in having a sundae bar at my son's graduation party in the spring."

"Wonderful!" Anna said. "Call me anytime."

After all the guests had been served and those who wanted seconds returned, Anna and Todd began emptying the toppings back into their jars and loading them into the plastic boxes they had brought.

"Todd brought the leftover ice cream to the freezer downstairs," Anna said to Allie and Jackson. "I'll leave that here for the two of you."

"Awesome," Jackson said. "Wait here, and I'll get your check."

Chester wandered back up to the now-empty table. "Uncle Chester, your skin looks yellow. Are you feeling okay?" Allie asked, taking the bowl of ice cream from his hands.

"I'm getting a headache. Maybe I ate too much."

Allie put her hand on her uncle's forehead. "Your skin feels cold and clammy."

Chester leaned on the table. "I'm feeling a little lightheaded."

Allie walked Chester back to the couch, while Anna and Todd piled the boxes by the door. As Jackson returned and handed Anna a white envelope, a scream came from the living room. Anna turned and saw Chester on the floor with Violet kneeling over him.

Everyone turned toward Chester, who was clutching his throat.

"Help!" Violet cried.

Anna called 9-1-1, and within a few minutes, the paramedics were rushing Chester onto a stretcher and into an ambulance. He began to convulse as they wheeled him into the vehicle.

"I don't think this is what Allie and Jackson had in mind when they said they wanted to add some excitement to this party," Todd whispered to Anna.

CHAPTER 2

*a*s the ambulance drove away with Chester, two police officers arrived. They moved Allie's and Jackson's guests out of the house and taped off the surrounding area.

A few minutes later, Detective Charlie Doyle pulled up. He parked on the street and walked somberly toward one of the police officers who was already on the scene. Charlie stopped short when he saw Anna, holding a box filled with ice cream toppings.

He shook his head, and Anna thought she saw a smirk form on the corners of his lips. "I should have known you'd be here, Anna McBride. You know the drill. I'll need you to stay here until I have a chance to question everyone." Charlie turned to the guests. "In fact, I'll need everyone to stay here until we can get your statements."

"I can't stay here!" Violet said. "I have to get to the hospital. My husband is sick, and I need to be with him. He shouldn't be alone right now."

Charlie pulled Violet around to the side of the house. The

stunned silence that had settled on the group was broken by a high-pitched shriek. "It can't be! It can't be!" Violet repeated.

Allie and Nick jogged toward Charlie and Violet, presumably to comfort Violet. Shortly after, Charlie reappeared in the front yard. "I'm sorry to have to tell you this, folks, but Chester passed away on the way to the hospital."

There was a collective gasp.

"Anna, I understand Chester complained about the hot fudge. I'm going to have to take your fudge with me to test it and make sure there was nothing in it that caused Chester's death."

"Of course," Anna said. "But most of the people here, including Todd and me, had some of that hot fudge. If it were the fudge, everyone would be sick."

"That's probably true, but we need to check it, anyway. What happened to the sundae that Chester complained about?"

"He ate about half of it, but after he complained, we threw it away and gave him a caramel one instead," Anna said. "The trash barrel is in the house."

Charlie motioned for Anna to follow him inside. "Show me."

Todd followed, and Charlie didn't object.

Anna led Charlie to the folding table that had been a festive sundae bar a little while before. "There was a trash receptacle right here," Anna said.

"I think I saw Jackson move it into the kitchen while we were packing up," Todd said.

Charlie and Anna followed Todd into the kitchen. It was a large kitchen for a small home. Anna guessed that either Allie and Jackson or the previous owners had expanded it from its original size. There was a long row of white cabinets, divided in the middle by a double window above the farmer's sink, overlooking a sizeable backyard. Attached to the kitchen was a small butler's pantry, with another row of upper and lower cabinets and a water cooler.

"There's the trash," Anna said, pointing to a bucket next to a spacious blue island with white and grey quartz countertops. "It's in there, somewhere. Fortunately, we used paper bowls, so Chester's sundae is in the trash bucket and not in the garbage disposal."

"It should be easy enough to find," Todd said. "It's the only bowl that still has ice cream left in it. Everyone else cleaned their bowls."

Charlie slipped on a pair of plastic gloves and sorted through the trash until he pulled up the mixture of melted fudge, vanilla ice cream, and toppings.

He placed it in a bag and left the kitchen, presumably to bring it to a police officer.

"I'm sorry I got you into this, Todd," Anna said. "You know the old saying: 'No good deed goes unpunished.'"

"Don't worry about me," Todd said. "But poor Chester. It seems like the police believe he was poisoned. Who do you think…"

Anna cut Todd off. "Todd, look at this!" She held up a jar of hot fudge. "It was hidden behind the spice rack."

"That doesn't look familiar. I don't think it's one of the jars we packed," Todd said.

"*Definitely* not. I don't use this brand." Anna opened the cap and sniffed the jar's contents. "It's hot fudge, but it has a bitter smell."

She held it up for Todd to sniff. "You're right. What is that?"

"It reminds me of almonds." Anna looked at the ingredients printed on the label. "It doesn't say anything about almonds."

Charlie returned to the kitchen, and Anna handed him the jar. "If this was what was used to poison Chester, the killer could have brought this hot fudge and put it on Chester's sundae, on top of the fudge that was already on it. Maybe that's why Chester's sundae was the only one that tasted strange," Anna said.

Charlie sniffed the jar. "You're right. There's a faint scent of almonds. Could be arsenic. But that wouldn't explain the convulsions or the strange taste that Chester complained about. Maybe it's arsenic mixed with something else. Strychnine perhaps. That would have caused a bitter taste, and it would explain the convulsions. We won't know for sure until the test results come back. I'll need the two of you to stick around for a while."

Anna nodded.

"No problem," Todd said.

Then he and Anna went back outside where the others were waiting to give their statements.

Allie, Jackson, and Drake came right over to Anna and Todd. Allie begged Anna to tell them what had happened while they were inside, and Anna didn't have the heart to refuse her request.

Allie put her hand over her mouth when she heard about the possibility of poison. "And we dismissed him, thinking he was just being difficult."

"Don't be so hard on yourself," Drake said. "Uncle Chester

complained about everything today. How were you supposed to know that he was for real this time?"

"But still," Allie said, "if we had called the paramedics sooner, he might still be alive."

"Seriously, Allie, Drake is right. If we called the paramedics every time Chester complained about something, he'd be in the hospital every day," Nick said wryly.

Jackson put his arm around Allie. "They're right. This is nobody's fault."

Anna looked around the yard. It was *somebody's* fault. And she knew from experience that everyone at the party would be a person of interest.

Allie and Jackson tried to comfort their guests, while Anna and Todd watched, unsure of what to do.

Eliza and Dorothea came and stood beside them.

"What an awful party this turned out to be," Dorothea said.

"I don't believe we've officially met." Anna extended her hand to Dorothea. "I'm Anna McBride, and this is Todd Devonshire."

"Dorothea," the woman said.

"We met earlier when I took one of Anna's business cards for Bret's graduation party in the spring," Eliza explained to Dorothea. Then she turned toward Anna and Todd. "Dorothea and I are both friends of Violet's."

"We both watched Allie grow up," Dorothea said.

"Allie's parents passed away in a car accident five years ago, but when Allie was younger, she and her mother would visit Chester at his office from time to time," Eliza added.

"Poor Allie," Anna said. "She lost her parents, and now her uncle."

"Allie always did everything she could to keep Chester in

her life, even though he was, let's say, challenging. Allie's mother, Joy, was nothing like her brother, except in physical appearance. I think Allie enjoyed being with him because of the physical resemblance to her mother. And because her mother seemed to love him."

"And back then, Chester wasn't quite as crabby," Dorothea added. "I think it changed him when he lost his sister."

"You know, I think you're right," Eliza said. "I never thought of that, but now that you mention it, he did change after Joy died."

"Violet feels the same way," Dorothea said. "I think she was always hoping he'd become more like his old self again one day."

Violet began sobbing again a few feet away, so the two women excused themselves. "We should get back to our friend," Dorothea said.

"Of course," Anna said.

Todd glanced around. "It feels a bit intrusive to be here."

"I agree, but Charlie told us not to leave until he could talk to us."

"I saw an oak tree out back with two turquoise Adirondack chairs underneath. Let's wait over there," Todd suggested.

Anna and Todd walked toward the oak tree, which was ablaze with the colors of fall.

Anna kicked up a pile of leaves while they walked. "Fallen leaves always make me feel like a little kid again."

Todd also kicked up a few leaves. "I know what you mean."

Anna couldn't help but laugh. She had never seen him act like a kid.

They sat in the Adirondack chairs and waited for Charlie.

"Not that I'm trying to make a pitch for business," Todd said, "but since we're just sitting here, I was thinking. You might want to start investing some of your summer profits. I know you said that you would rather wait until after the slow season, but we could move a modest amount of your profits into a tax-deferred retirement account so you could avoid paying so many taxes. It would save you money in the long run."

Anna thought about Todd's suggestion for a moment. "Thanks, Todd. What you're saying makes a lot of sense, but I think I'll wait until next year to do that. I'm a bit risk averse with my finances, and I still don't know how much of those profits I'll need to carry me through the spring. I don't want to close the shop in January, because that wouldn't be fair to my employees. But by next fall, I'll be ready to start doing something like that."

"I understand," Todd said. "You have to feel comfortable and ready before making a financial commitment like that."

Just as Anna and Todd were running out of things to talk about, Charlie came and sat on the grass in front of them.

Todd stood up and offered his chair, but Charlie said he didn't mind the grass.

Anna and Todd relayed in detail everything that happened from the moment they arrived.

"Someone had to have put the infected hot fudge onto Chester's sundae, but who?" Anna asked.

"Did either of you notice anybody tamper with Chester's ice cream? Or even be alone with him?" Charlie asked.

They both shook their heads.

"We were busy serving all those guests. I honestly didn't see a thing, Charlie. All I can tell you is that Allie and Jackson

17

stood next to Todd and me greeting guests the whole time, so it couldn't have been either of them. Chester's wife, Violet was close by his side, but I do remember her talking with Jackson when we first arrived, so she wasn't with him constantly. I wish we could be more helpful. Did the other guests see anything?"

"Apparently, after Chester got his sundae, he went into the kitchen to get some water. Since the jar of fudge that you found was in the kitchen, it was likely then that the sundae was poisoned. That is, assuming the tests from your fudge come back negative. But since nobody else got sick, I'm assuming they will."

"There was a butler's pantry attached to the kitchen, and it had a water cooler. Chester could have put down his sundae when he went into the pantry to get some water. Maybe that's when the killer did it."

"None of the guests saw anyone else going into the kitchen with Chester?" Todd asked.

"People were popping in and out of there, since the drinks were in the kitchen, but nobody noticed anyone tampering with Chester's sundae. We're still interviewing witnesses, but I have a feeling it won't be that easy."

"I'm sorry we couldn't be any more help," Anna said.

"I know where to find you if any other questions come up. And Todd, I'll take your phone number, as well, in case I need to reach you."

"Of course," Todd said, pulling out a business card from his wallet and handing it to Charlie. "My cell phone number is on there."

Anna and Todd said goodbye to Allie and Jackson before leaving. Anna and the young couple had already exchanged phone numbers because of the party, but Todd also did the same. "If there's anything you need, please don't hesitate to ask."

"That goes for me, too," Anna said.

Then, Anna and Todd drove back to *Bella's Dream*.

CHAPTER 3

"*W*hat an afternoon," Todd said as the two brought the boxes into the storage room at *Bella's Dream.*

"I'll bet you regret coming in for an ice cream today," Anna said.

Todd laughed and shook his head. "I certainly got more than I bargained for. But no, I don't regret it. I should get going, though. I have a few errands to run, including a trip to the grocery store. I'm down to a bottle of seltzer water and a few eggs."

"Of course. Thanks for everything, Todd. Today would have been a lot harder if I had been alone. And I mean both the sundae bar and the aftermath."

He winked at Anna. "My pleasure. I'll see you soon."

"By the way, I owe you a hot fudge sundae. The next time you come in, your sundae is on me."

"It's a deal."

Anna quickly unpacked the plastic boxes, put them on a shelf for future use, then checked in with her employees.

Foot traffic on Main Street was significantly lighter in October than during the summer months, but the leaf peepers still brought in a steady flow of customers, especially on weekends. September had been busier than Anna expected, thanks to the lingering warm, sunny days. But this meant she hadn't had time to continue her search for her sister. She still had a list of salons that Joe Wiggins had compiled for her in August, and she was anxious to get started. Anna made a mental note to call Jeremy Russo that evening to take him up on his offer to accompany her on her trips to Maine.

Since Anna's employees had everything under control, she brought her car back to her cottage. This way, she would be able to walk home at the end of the evening to get some exercise and fresh air. It also gave her a chance to grab a quick bite to eat, since she had skipped lunch.

When Anna returned, she spent her time out front, mostly socializing with customers while her employees worked the counter.

In the early evening, after the post-dinner rush, a tired-looking Allie and Jackson trudged into *Bella's Dream*.

Anna took off her apron and brought them to a booth in the adjacent dining room.

"I've been thinking about the two of you ever since I left. How are you doing?"

Allie shrugged. "We've been better."

"It was a heck of a way to celebrate our first wedding anniversary," Jackson said. "Poor Violet. She's a hot mess."

"Have the two of you given any thought to who did this to your uncle?" Anna asked. "We won't know for sure until the tests on the fudge come back, but the police seem to be leaning towards foul play. That means that somebody at your party likely added the poisoned hot fudge to Chester's sundae."

"The police do seem to be leaning toward that theory," Jackson agreed.

Allie tucked a lock of curly blond hair behind her ears. "Uncle Chester sure had a way of getting under people's skin. As you saw at the party, he complained about everything and criticized everyone. But I don't think there was anyone who wanted to kill him," Allie said.

"There was at least one person who wanted to kill him," Jackson said. "And that person went to a lot of effort to do that."

Anna had been thinking the same thing, but she was glad that Jackson articulated that difficult truth first. As Anna thought about what happened, she felt a surge of anger toward the killer. Whoever did this not only took a man's life, and ruined a special moment for Allie and Jackson, but they used Anna's hot fudge sundae bar to do it. Chester's death was beginning to feel personal.

"Did the police tell you whether they have any suspects?" Anna asked.

"They didn't say. They questioned everyone at the party, but we weren't privy to those conversations. I guess it's too soon to speculate," Jackson said.

"You're right. These things take time," Anna said. "There's still a lot of legwork and questioning that have to happen before they get a clear picture."

"We feel really badly to have dragged you into this, Anna," Allie said. "We thought we were doing a good thing by having a hot fudge sundae bar."

"You have nothing to apologize for. I was thrilled to do it, and you had no way of knowing the day would end in tragedy."

"We still feel responsible," Jackson said. "We hope it won't stop people from hiring you for similar events in the future. We know you are trying to expand your offerings during the off season."

Anna looked at the earnest young couple. "I don't want the two of you to worry about that. This had nothing to do with you. Although, I have to admit, I am pretty upset with whoever the killer is."

"Still. If there's anything we can do to make it up to you, please let us know," Allie said.

Anna took a deep breath. Then she asked the question she had wanted to ask since Chester was pronounced dead. "Since you mentioned it, would you mind if I did a little investigating myself? I seem to have a knack for solving murders in this town, and I'd like to know sooner rather than later who did this."

They both looked at Anna, as if waiting for her to elaborate.

"Really?" Jackson asked, while Anna was still trying to figure out how to explain the fact that she repeatedly got sucked into solving murders ever since she moved to Seagull Cove. "How did you ever get involved in investigating murders?"

Anna smiled. "It's a long story."

"I don't mind," Allie said. "It certainly can't hurt to have someone else looking into things."

"I agree," Jackson said. "We're happy to help you in any way we can."

Anna leaned back in the booth and posed her earlier question one more time. "I know it's hard to imagine one of your guests being a killer," she began. "But Jackson is right. *Somebody* at the party did it. Nobody could have snuck into your house with all those people. They would have had to pass through the living room to get to the kitchen, where it appears Chester's sundae was poisoned. It had to have been an invited guest. Who has a grudge against your uncle that could warrant such drastic measures?"

Allie looked at Jackson and took a deep breath. "As much as I hate to admit it, my cousin, Drake, and my uncle, Nick, have always had a rocky relationship with Uncle Chester. He was particularly hard on both of them. Uncle Chester and Aunt Violet married later in life, and they don't have any children. Besides Aunt Violet, his only heirs are Uncle Nick and my cousins. I think that's the only reason Drake and Uncle Nick put up with Uncle Chester's demeaning attitude and blatant manipulation."

"So that they wouldn't get cut from the will?"

Allie nodded. "There are only three of us cousins. Myself, Drake, and Drake's brother, Oliver. Oliver and his family are away on vacation, which is why they couldn't make our anniversary party."

"Drake is the one who looked like a wannabe professor?" Anna asked.

Allie chuckled. "More like a wannabe famous author."

"Hey, his first book was pretty good," Jackson said. "And the sequel just came out this week. I'm actually going to pick up a copy."

"So, he *is* an author?" Anna asked.

"Yes. But we were never allowed to talk about Drake's books in front of Uncle Chester."

"Why not?"

"Because Drake always wanted to be a writer, but Uncle Chester threatened to cut him out of the will if he didn't study something more lucrative," Allie explained. "He claimed he didn't want Drake to be a nobody like his father. Uncle Chester believed an author career was just a pipe dream. So, Drake studied law and became a patent attorney, but he writes books on the side. In a weird way, I think Uncle Chester thought he was helping Drake by making him take a more reliable job, but his plan backfired. Drake is more passionate about his writing now than ever. And he was determined to succeed so he would no longer need Uncle Chester's money. He couldn't wait for the day he made his own fortune so he could rub it in his uncle's face."

"But Violet was his wife. Wouldn't she get most of his money?" Anna asked.

"She would certainly inherit a lot of it. But Uncle Chester was a shrewd businessman, so there was plenty to go around. He left a fair amount to us kids in his will, and he made sure we didn't forget that."

"It's kind of sad," Jackson said. "I think Chester was afraid nobody would want to spend time with him, so he lorded his fortune over everyone. He always found a way to remind them that they were in his will when he wanted something."

"I also noticed some tension between Nick and Chester," Anna said.

Allie nodded. "He and Uncle Chester had a touch-and-go relationship. From what my mom told me when she was alive, they could never see eye-to-eye on anything, ever since they were kids. Maybe their problems went deeper than I realized. Maybe Uncle Nick wanted Uncle Chester out of the picture, both for his boys' sakes and his." Allie looked up at Jackson, as if she were realizing something for the first time. "I can't believe Uncle Nick is the only one left of my mother and her siblings."

Jackson put his arm around his wife's shoulders. "I'm sorry, honey."

"We're meeting with Drake tomorrow afternoon," Allie said. "Why don't you join us? You could ask him some questions if you're serious about investigating."

"I'd like that," Anna said.

"I'll let you know when and where. We're staying in a hotel tonight, since our home is still a crime scene. Hopefully we'll be able to get back in tomorrow."

Allie and Jackson left, and Anna decided to call it a day. She reminded her staff to feed Casper, and then she walked home.

The evenings were getting chilly, so Anna put on her fleece sweatshirt and took the long way home to clear her head. While she was walking, she called Jeremy.

Jeremy didn't even bother to say 'hello.' He answered by saying, "Please don't tell me that you were hosting the hot fudge sundae bar at the anniversary party this afternoon."

"How'd you know?" Anna asked.

"As soon as I heard that the victim might have been killed with poisoned hot fudge, I had a hunch. No offense, but you do have a propensity for being nearby whenever someone is murdered in Seagull Cove."

"None taken. Unfortunately, I was there. But that's not why I was calling."

"Let me guess. You're ready to start venturing out to some of those nail salons on the list Joe put together for you."

"Right again. Things have slowed down in the shop, so I'd love to get started."

"Let's do it. How many salons are on the list?"

"Nineteen. I've broken them down by region, so we can hit several in one day. I figured we could start with the towns closest to home."

"Sounds like a good plan. I have Monday off."

"Perfect. Let's plan on Monday."

"Okay. Since a murder just took place, I'll have to go into the newsroom first, just to make sure nothing major is about to break. But I'll plan on picking you up at 10:00."

"Okay, great. See you then."

CHAPTER 4

*A*nna attended a later Mass on Sunday morning so she could sleep in, then went into *Bella's Dream.* Grey clouds fanned out across the sky over Seagull Cove, giving the town the appearance of being in mourning after another murder.

When Anna turned on her phone after Mass, there was a text message from Allie. *The police let us return home this morning. Drake will be here at 2:00. Can you still come?*

Anna let Allie know that she would be there. She left work at 1:45 to ensure she would arrive before Drake did.

It was an eerie feeling entering the house, where a man had been murdered just over twenty-four hours before.

Drake stopped short on his way into the living room, where Anna, Allie, and Jackson were seated.

"I don't mean to be rude, but I thought it would just be family. No offense," Drake said to Anna.

"None taken," Anna said.

"Anna has a talent for solving tough mysteries, so we invited her, too," Allie said.

"We're still in shock that someone did this to Chester in our own home," Jackson added. "We hoped Anna could provide some perspective as we try to figure out what happened."

Drake quickly regained his composure. "Of course. That's a good idea. We all want to know what happened to Uncle Chester. It's nice to see you again, Anna. I'm sorry you had to be present yesterday for that horrible scene."

"I'm just sorry that happened to one of your family members," Anna said.

Drake looked at Allie. "Would you believe that the police questioned both Oliver and Cheryl last night?"

"Oliver and Cheryl are Drake's brother and sister-in-law," Jackson explained to Anna.

"I guess because us cousins are in Uncle Chester's will, we are all suspects," Drake said. "And apparently your spouses, too, since they would also stand to gain from Uncle Chester's death. I guess that's one good thing about being single."

"Please tell me that someone told Oliver and Cheryl about Chester's death before the police called them," Anna said.

Drake nodded. "Of course. My father and I called him as soon as we finished talking with the police yesterday. Jackson and Allie called his friends so that Aunt Violet wouldn't have to do it. Most of them were at the party, so there weren't a lot of calls to make. Uncle Chester didn't exactly have a lot of friends," he added.

"I'm glad to hear they heard the news from loved ones," Anna said.

"Fortunately for Oliver and Cheryl, they both had solid alibis. They were on vacation, and the whole family was together in a restaurant at the time it happened. So, as far as the cousins and their spouses go, I guess it's just the three of us who are left on the old suspect list," Drake said.

"Sorry, Drake," Jackson said. "Allie and I were standing next to Anna greeting our guests as they came up for a sundae. We were there up until Chester collapsed. We've been cleared, as well."

"Good for you guys. Not that I ever suspected you. I guess Aunt Violet, my father, and I can expect more visits from the police, since we are the only ones left to gain financially from his death."

Anna studied Drake. He didn't seem like a grieving nephew.

Drake seemed to have read Anna's thoughts. "I'm sorry about the guy's death. Truly I am. That is a terrible thing to have happened to anyone, even to a guy like Uncle Chester, who lived to make others' lives miserable. But I would never kill the guy. He *was* my father's brother."

"What about the other people in your family?" Anna wanted to ask about Nick, but she was waiting for the right moment.

"Well, there's Aunt Violet," Drake said. "She is his primary beneficiary."

"You can't possibly believe that she is capable of murder?" Allie asked.

Drake shrugged his shoulders. "She did have to live with the man. I don't know how she lasted sixteen years living under the same roof as him. She's either a saint, or she snapped and just couldn't take it anymore. Maybe both."

"I know that I'm the one who brought us all together today, but I don't like suspecting members of my family," Allie said. "My mother wouldn't like this conversation one bit if she were here."

"I know, Allie. But someone at our party killed Chester," Jackson said. "I know it's unpleasant to think about, but we have to face the facts."

"Isn't it possible that the killer wasn't an invited guest to the party?" Drake asked. "Uncle Chester, being, well, Uncle Chester, has made his share of enemies over the years. Maybe it was a disgruntled client or another acquaintance."

"That's not possible," Anna said. "The only time Chester put down his sundae was when he went into the kitchen for some water. That has to be when the killer poured the poisoned hot fudge onto Chester's sundae. There is no entrance to the kitchen from outside, and there were no uninvited guests spotted at the party. There's no way anyone could have snuck in undetected."

"That's right," Jackson said. "There are only two entrances to the house. One is through the front door, and the other is through the garage, which was closed yesterday."

"Nobody could have gone unnoticed in here," Allie said. "The killer had to have been a guest."

"There were twenty-three people at the party," Allie said. "Of those twenty-three people, most of them barely knew Uncle Chester. They were either friends of ours who live in the area or Jackson's family. Most of them would have no motive whatsoever to kill him."

"It was obviously someone who knew Chester," Anna said. "Could you guys make a list of the people present at the party who knew your uncle? That will give us a place to start."

"Sure. We'll make a list and bring it to the ice cream shop

later," Allie said. "After our visit with Drake, the three of us are planning to pay a visit to Aunt Violet. We thought we'd keep her company for a little while."

"Well, I, for one, plan to leave the sleuthing to the police," Drake said. "I think it's crazy for you to be getting involved. Whoever did this is a dangerous person, and frankly, Uncle Chester probably invited it upon himself. I don't mean to sound callous, but those are the facts. It's not worth my life."

"I'll leave the three of you to visit," Anna said. "But before I leave, who do you think did it, Drake?"

"I don't know. There are as many motives as people who know Uncle Chester. But I'll tell you who my father thinks did it."

Anna, Allie, and Jackson looked wide-eyed at Drake.

"Eliza," he said, sounding as if he had the gossip of the century.

"Chester's secretary?" Anna asked.

"Hasn't she worked for Chester for ages?" Jackson asked.

"Pretty much," Allie said. "More than fifteen years."

"Why would *she* kill him?" Anna asked.

Drake scoffed. "I'd want to kill him if I had to work for him every day for fifteen years."

"There would have to be more of a reason than that," Anna said. "If Eliza was unhappy working for Chester, she could have just quit."

"True," Drake said. "But if that were the case, my father wouldn't have suggested that." He whipped out his phone. "Let's ask him."

Drake tapped a few times on his phone, and Nick picked up the phone right away.

"Hi, Dad, it's me. I'm sitting here at Allie's house with Allie,

Jackson, and Anna. Yes, the hot fudge sundae lady." Drake winked at Anna. "We're discussing what happened to Uncle Chester. I know you said you think Eliza did it, but why? Uh huh. Oh, yeah, I see what you mean. Typical Uncle Chester. Thanks, Dad. I'll see you later."

Drake disconnected the call.

"What did he say?" Jackson asked.

"My dad thinks Eliza did it, all right. He said that Eliza has been wanting to leave forever, but my uncle wouldn't let her. He doesn't know why she didn't just quit. He thinks Uncle Chester was holding something over her."

"Maybe he threatened to give her a bad recommendation?"

"It seems to me like she still could leave," Anna said. "What difference would one recommendation make?"

"It may not have been that easy. This is the only job Eliza has held in fifteen years. She gained a little experience as a secretary after she graduated high school, but soon after, she married her late husband and started a family. She didn't work again until after her husband passed away. It was then that she went to work for Uncle Chester. I remember my mother saying that perhaps her brother was turning over a new leaf and becoming more charitable, after he gave Eliza a chance."

Drake scoffed. "Aunt Joy should have known better than that. There was always an angle with that man. He probably knew he could more easily manipulate her, because she needed the job. She's still several years away from retirement. She probably figured she couldn't handle even one more year with that man."

"You could be right," Anna said. "If her back was against a

wall, maybe she took drastic measures. Poison is often the murder method of choice for women."

"I guess that makes sense," Allie said. "It's less confrontational and doesn't depend on physical strength."

"I should get back to work," Anna said. "I'll leave the two of you to your visit."

CHAPTER 5

*a*nna glanced at the blue house as she started her car. The balloons hung deflated from the railing and the "Happy Anniversary" banner, which had been fastened across the front porch, was lifeless on the floor. Even the leaves on the oak tree in the back yard seemed duller than when she saw it for the first time the previous afternoon.

Back at *Bella's Dream,* Joe Wiggins had just arrived for his daily two scoops. His tan had only slightly faded due to the unseasonable warm September they had enjoyed.

"Joe, I have a new fall ice cream flavor for you to sample. One of the reps from *Finnegan's Creamery* has been trying to convince me to carry it, so I decided to give it a try this fall. I'll give you two scoops on the house in exchange for an honest opinion. Are you game to take a chance?"

"What's the flavor?"

"Maple walnut," Anna said.

"Oooh, yes, I'm definitely game."

She put two generous scoops in a glass dish and slid it in front of Joe, who took his usual seat at the counter.

"I'm about ready for a change from my usual chocolate chip." He put a spoonful in his mouth. "And I think I just found my new fall flavor."

"That makes it unanimous. The staff likes it, too. I'll put up a sign and start to promote it."

"How are things going with Bella's investigation?" Joe asked between spoons of ice cream.

"It's funny you should ask. I haven't had a chance to follow up on the list you gave me in August, but I did just speak with Jeremy. We have plans to visit a few of the salons tomorrow. You're welcome to join us," Anna said.

Joe crinkled his nose. "Sounds like a lot of busy work. I think I'll let you and Jeremy handle this part. But I'll look forward to hearing how things progress."

In August, Jeremy and Anna visited *Castleton Beauty School*, where they suspected Bella had attended. When Anna showed their tour guide, Justine, a picture of Bella, she recognized her immediately and called her Izzy, which is a nickname Bella could very well be using, since her full name was Isabel. Justine quickly took back her words and denied that she had ever met Bella, but it was too late. Justine's initial reaction to seeing Bella's photo was all the confirmation that Anna needed that her sister had indeed attended *Castleton*.

Joe had managed to get Anna a list of nail salons where the graduates of *Castleton* had obtained employment. There was no guarantee that Bella was at one of those salons, but at least it was a place to start.

"Hopefully, even if we don't find Bella, we can talk with someone who knew her and who can point us in the right direction," Anna said.

Of course, Anna really hoped she would walk into one of those salons and find her sister sitting there. In her daydreams, Anna would throw her arms around Bella, and her sister would say something like, "I never should have staged my death. I'm coming home, and we'll figure this out together." But Anna didn't dare say that aloud. It would be like announcing your wish after you blew out your birthday candles. Even if you weren't superstitious, you just didn't do it.

Joe finished his maple walnut ice cream and chatted with the staff before leaving.

"Good luck tomorrow, kiddo," he said on his way out.

Anna went into her office to create a sign, advertising their new ice cream flavor. While she waited for it to print, she glanced at the calendar of events for the month of October. She had scheduled an open mic night for Thursday evenings, which was becoming a tradition. It brought people into the shop, and they, of course, bought ice cream. She also added a regular karaoke night, which was also catching on. Then she had a few musicians coming in on various nights. But Anna would need to be creative to get customers into an ice cream shop as the days got colder. She had been hoping to advertise her hot fudge sundae bars for private events, but now she hesitated. People likely heard what happened at Allie's and Jackson's anniversary party. "I'd better wait until this murder is solved," she said to herself.

While Anna was posting the sign on the door, Allie and Jackson came in. They each ordered an ice cream cone, and Anna sat with them in the adjoining dining room.

"How is Violet doing?" Anna asked.

"She's quite upset," Allie said.

Jackson looked at Allie with raised eyebrows. "We agreed to tell Anna the truth."

Allie let out a sigh. "Oh, all right. But I still don't believe she killed my uncle. The truth is, she was quite shaken up yesterday, but she seems to have quickly recovered. I'm ashamed of the way my family has been behaving since this whole thing happened. Aunt Violet was planning the services, practically humming as she assigned each of us tasks. She already brought up the will twice. And then there's Drake."

"He did seem a bit callous to me over the whole thing," Anna said.

"He got even worse while we were at Aunt Violet's. It was like the two of them fed off each other. And then Uncle Nick showed up. I thought at least he would reprimand Drake, but he didn't even seem to notice. Someone poisoned Uncle Chester, and nobody in our family seems at all concerned with figuring out what happened. We were trying to get them to speculate, but all they seem to care about is getting their inheritance and planning what they were going to do next. Uncle Chester hasn't even been buried yet!"

Jackson didn't seem as surprised by the situation as Allie was.

"It sounds like they are all somewhat relieved that he is out of their lives," Anna said.

"I would have hoped for a little more respect," Allie said.

Anna didn't want to hurt Allie, but there was no way of putting it delicately. "I know it seems insensitive, but unless they all killed him together, which is highly unlikely, perhaps people just felt that way about him. Maybe their behavior doesn't have anything to do with having killed him."

"Everyone couldn't have disliked him *that* much," Allie said.

Jackson squeezed Allie's hand. "I know you loved him, because your mother did. But you didn't have to live or work with the man, and he didn't try to control your life the way he did Drake's. He knew he couldn't use his money to manipulate you, like he did Nick and Drake."

"So, you think Aunt Violet, Uncle Nick, or Drake did it?" Allie asked.

"Or Eliza," Jackson said. "We all knew that Chester was growing even more impossible to be around, and Aunt Violet and Eliza were likely taking the brunt of it. We also know that Drake allowed himself to be manipulated over the inheritance, while you never did. And then there's Nick. After all these years, he still put up with Chester's insults. Maybe one of them couldn't take it anymore."

"Is there anyone else at the party besides Violet, Nick, Eliza, and Drake who had a motive?" Anna asked.

Allie fished a piece of paper from her pocket. "I made a list of everyone who was at the party, like I promised. I crossed out those who barely knew Uncle Chester. It's safe to say none of our friends and nobody in Jackson's family did it."

Anna counted up the names. "That only leaves five people out of the original twenty-three who were at the party."

"That's right," Allie said. "I included Dorothea on the list, but I can't think of a motive for her."

"We'll keep her on the list for now. She may have a motive that we haven't discovered yet. How close was Dorothea to Violet?"

"She was one of Aunt Violet's best friends."

"Could she have wanted him out of the picture because of

the way he treated Violet?" Anna asked. "It seems to be the consensus that Chester's difficult behavior grew worse over the years."

"We always knew she would do anything for Aunt Violet, but murder? That seems like a stretch," Allie said.

"We're going to check in on Violet again tomorrow," Jackson said. "Perhaps you should come along with us and ask her yourself."

"I'd love to, but I can't come tomorrow. What about Tuesday?" Anna asked.

"That would work, too," Allie said. "We're going to make it a point to visit her every day until the funeral to make sure she's okay and to see if she needs more help with the funeral arrangements."

"Okay. Let's touch base on Tuesday and arrange a time to meet," Anna said.

"We'd better get going. We're exhausted. It's been a long couple of days," Allie said.

After they left, Anna decided to follow their lead. She had a big day planned for visiting salons tomorrow.

There was a chill in the air, so when Anna got home, she changed into her baby blue fleece pullover and her softest pair of jeans, and brewed an oversized mug of apple cinnamon tea. She took it to the porch to enjoy a few more minutes of fresh air. She imagined that she wouldn't be able to sit outside for much longer with the cold weather on its way, so she relished the time outdoors.

Wanda pulled into the driveway next door. She waved when she spotted Anna.

Ever since Wanda had come to Anna's for tea in August, she had been more at ease in Anna's presence. She sometimes came outside to keep Anna company when she was sitting on her porch. This time, she only waved and exchanged a few pleasantries before going inside.

Anna often had the feeling that Wanda had more that she wanted to say, as if she carried something just beneath the surface that she wanted to talk about. But she never seemed to be able to open up.

CHAPTER 6

*A*nna was barely able to sleep on Sunday night, knowing that she and Jeremy would begin visiting nail salons and searching for Bella the following day. She woke up long before her alarm went off, so she put on a warm sweatshirt and took a walk along Mile Long Beach to pass the time.

She relished the warmth of the sun on her face while she walked. It shone brightly even though it was only fifty-five degrees. Anna stopped and sat on the wall, saying a prayer that she would find some answers today. She pulled from her pocket the list of salons that Joe had compiled. She had divided the twenty-three salons into four groups of three to four, based on proximity, and circled each group with a different colored pen. Today was the red group. She and Jeremy would visit three nail salons, all located in or near Kennebunk.

A friendly voice pulled her from her thoughts. "Hi, Anna. I thought that was you."

It was Wanda's husband, Daniel, sitting on the wraparound porch of his large Victorian home and sipping from a hunter green mug.

"Oh, hi, Daniel. I didn't see you there."

He smirked. "I can tell. You looked absorbed in whatever you were looking at."

"Oh, it's my list of things to do for the day."

"It must be quite a list. You look like you have the weight of the world on your shoulders."

Anna smiled. "I suppose there are a few important tasks on here. No work today?" Wanda had told Anna last month that Daniel was a doctor who owned a private practice.

"I'll be going in a little later. I've been cutting back on hours and leaving the practice in my young colleague's capable hands." He smiled warmly. "I'll leave you to solve the world's problems."

Just the problems in my *world*, Anna thought.

She continued on her walk, and when she got home, it was still only 9:30. So, she sat on the couch looking out the front window and anxiously awaited Jeremy's arrival.

When he pulled into the driveway, Anna was out the door before he had a chance to beep his car horn.

"That was fast," Jeremy said when Anna hopped into the passenger's seat.

"I guess I'm a little anxious to get this search started."

"So, where are we headed first, boss?" Jeremy asked.

Anna smiled. "First up is *Katie's Nail Salon*. It's in Kennebunk, not too far from *Castleton Beauty School*."

She read Jeremy the address, and he tapped it into the GPS application on his phone.

"I can't even remember what we used to do in the old days, before these machines," Anna said.

"I seem to remember always having books of maps in my trunk. Now I just have to make sure I have my phone charger."

They hopped onto Route 95 North and were off to their first salon.

Although Anna's mind was occupied with thinking of possible scenarios of what might happen if they found Bella that day, she still couldn't help but admire the beautiful colors as they drove north.

"Have you thought about what you're going to say when we get there?" Jeremy asked. "Judging from our experience with Justine at *Castleton*, it's obvious Bella has told people she doesn't want to be found."

"I was thinking the same thing. My plan is to say that I had a great experience with a technician named Izzy when I was visiting a friend in town, and now that I'm back, I was hoping to book an appointment with her again. I'll say I couldn't remember the salon I went to and was hoping this was the place."

"That might work. They'll have no reason to hide her identity if they believe you're looking for her for professional reasons."

At 11:45 they pulled into the parking lot of *Katie's Nail Salon*.

"Would you like me to come in, or am I just here for moral support?" Jeremy asked.

"I'd rather you come in. Maybe you'll notice something that I don't."

They exited the car and walked into *Katie's Nail Salon*. Anna immediately scanned the salon looking for Bella, but she wasn't in the room. There were a couple of women getting pedicures, another getting a manicure, and in the back was a group of technicians sitting and chatting.

"May I help you?" one of the women giving a pedicure, asked.

"I hope so. My name is Anna, and I got a manicure from a technician named Izzy when I was visiting my friend over the summer. I can't remember the salon I went to, so I was wondering if she happens to work here. I was hoping to book another appointment with her now that I'm back in town."

The woman shook her head. "No Izzy here, but we do give the best manicures in town." She gestured toward the group of women. "Any one of our technicians would take great care of you."

"Thank you, but I wanted to find Izzy. I promised I'd come back the next time I was in town. I believe she went to *Castleton Beauty School*. Do any of you happen to know her? She had long red hair and a great sense of humor."

One of the women spoke up. "I graduated from *Castleton* two years ago, but there was no Izzy there when I attended."

"I'll keep trying. Thanks, anyway," Anna said.

She and Jeremy left the salon.

"I guess we can cross that one off the list," Jeremy said.

Anna took out a pen and did just that when they got back into the car.

"Where to next?"

"*Nails 'R Us*," Anna said. "It's only a few miles away." She gave him the address, and off they went.

They had a similar experience at *Nails 'R Us*. Nobody knew a technician named Izzy, and none of them had been at *Castleton* at the same time as Bella.

"I know we've only been to two salons, but I hope every salon on this list doesn't turn out this way," Anna said.

"It's lunchtime," Jeremy said. "Let's stop for a quick bite before we hit the last one. Maybe a little food in your stomach will lift your spirits." Jeremy pointed to a large, white wooden structure with green trim that looked like a restored barn. "Look, there's a farm stand with an apple orchard. I'll bet we can get something good there."

The farmstand had rows of apples, peaches, berries, squash, zucchini, eggplant, tomatoes, carrots, and an array of other fresh fruits and vegetables. There was also a deli counter on the far side of the shop, where they each ordered a sandwich, a bag of chips, and fresh cider. Anna also bought some fresh veggies to take home. Then they found a bench under a maple tree. Anna inhaled the sweet air. "This was a great suggestion. I needed a break before we hit that last salon."

The fresh cider, along with Anna's turkey and avocado sandwich with fresh lettuce and tomato on warm bread, gave Anna the boost she needed. It was already mid-October, so the apple trees were picked bare. The young children playing by a pumpkin patch made Anna think of her family's trips to the orchard as a child. They would go every year in September to pick apples, then rush home to turn their spoils into bake goods. Apple crisp was Anna's favorite, but Bella liked baking pies. Anna and Bella had continued the tradition most years, even as adults.

The memories of Bella renewed Anna's energy even more than the food. When they finished eating, Jeremy plugged in the address to *The Seaside Salon,* and they were on their way once again.

"This one has a quaint name. I can imagine Bella being drawn to it."

Anna walked in and gave her story about looking for a technician named Izzy. As with the previous two salons, there was no technician named Izzy who worked there, so Anna asked if any of the girls had gone to *Castleton* and possibly knew Izzy from there.

The receptionist, whom Anna had been talking to, turned to a woman standing in the back. "Carly, you went to *Castleton*, didn't you?"

Carly smiled and nodded. "I did. Are you interested in enrolling?"

"No," Anna said. "I'm looking for a nail technician who graduated from there four years ago."

"Maybe I can help you. I was there around that time. What was her name?"

"Izzy," Anna said.

Carly's smile faded quickly.

"No, I don't know anyone by that name." She looked down at Anna's nails. "You don't look like you need a manicure, either. What are you up to?"

Anna was taken aback by Carly's abrupt response. The receptionist was equally surprised.

Anna could think of nothing to do but press forward. "Izzy had long red hair. She was funny. I'm sure you'd remember her."

"No, there was no Izzy at *Castleton* four years ago. You must be mistaken."

"But…"

"Excuse me, I have to get ready for my next appointment,"

Carly said, disappearing down the hallway in the back of the salon.

"I'm sorry. Please excuse Carly. I don't know what's gotten into her," the receptionist said.

Anna didn't know what to say.

Fortunately, Jeremy interjected. "That's okay. Everyone's entitled to a bad day." He put his hand on Anna's shoulder, and the two left *The Seaside Salon*.

CHAPTER 7

$\mathcal{A}$nna sat in silence for a moment in the passenger seat of Jeremy's car before speaking.

"That was the exact same reaction we got from Justine at *Castleton* when we asked about Bella," she finally said.

"I know. Carly clearly knew Bella, just like Justine did. But they are pretending not to."

"At least we're getting a consistent response," Anna said. "They obviously both knew her but pretended they didn't. It further confirms what we already knew. Bella went to *Castleton* four years ago, and she went to great lengths to conceal her identity."

"It's more than that," Jeremy said. "Both Carly and Justine looked at us as if we were a threat when we brought up her name. They are clearly trying to protect Bella."

"Bella obviously wouldn't have confided in people she barely knew about assuming a new identity," Anna said. "She must have come up with a story as to why she didn't want to be found."

"It seems that whatever story she came up with was

compelling enough so that her former classmates feel the need to protect her," Jeremy said. "We're going to have a hard time getting anyone who knew Bella from *Castleton* to point us in her direction, even if they know where she is."

"There's something else that's concerning me," Anna said. "If either Justine or Carly knows where to find Bella, she may know that I'm looking for her. That could make the search exponentially harder."

"I was thinking the same thing," Jeremy said. "But there's not much we can do about that. We have to ask around if we want to find her."

"You're right. We don't have any other leads to pursue. We have no choice but to continue to visit the salons on Joe's list and hope that she is at one of them. Or, at the very least, that someone will talk to us."

Jeremy paused and rubbed his chin. "Maybe you shouldn't bring up *Castleton* anymore. I doubt that anyone who knew Bella from that school will talk to us, anyway. I think we should continue visiting salons and asking about her, but don't mention *Castleton*. It seems to put people on the defensive."

Anna let out a sigh. She couldn't decide if she felt like she was closer to finding Bella or further away.

"Try to stay positive. Someone is bound to talk to us. It's a numbers game," Jeremy said.

"I know you're right. But I think I should change up my cover story. Now that I've said it aloud a few times, hunting around for a nail technician that I went to once before doesn't sound as convincing as I initially thought."

Jeremy thought for a moment. "How about if you say that you are planning a high school reunion, and Bella is a classmate? You could say that you heard she worked at a salon in the area."

"That could work. I'll say I'm in the neighborhood, because I'm visiting a friend from Maine, and I thought I'd ask around while I'm here."

"You might have better luck with a story like that. And don't mention *Castleton*. At all."

"I wish I knew the last name that Bella is using. That would make this search much easier."

"I agree," Jeremy said. "But we have to go with what we have. With a little luck, maybe someone will give us her last name."

Anna pulled her phone from her purse. "I just had an idea. Let me try a few searches using surnames in our family tree. Maybe she went with a familiar last name."

"It's worth a shot," Jeremy said.

Anna plugged in every surname she could think of and ran an internet search, along with the words 'Castleton,' 'nail technician,' and the names of the towns on their list.

After a few minutes, Anna shook her head. "It's no use."

"She probably used a name that was completely different to avoid being found," Jeremy said. "Don't forget, even if she never imagined that you'd go searching for her, she is trying to hide from *someone*. She would make it as hard as possible to be found."

Anna put her phone back in her pocket. "My head feels like it's going to explode from thinking so much. I'm glad that was the last stop of the day."

"Would you like to try again next Monday?" Jeremy asked. "Sundays and Mondays are my days off, but some of the salons will likely be closed on Sundays."

"Are you sure, Jeremy? I can't ask you to give up a day off every week. This investigation could take a while."

"I'm happy to come when I can. And I happen to be free on Monday."

"Okay. But don't feel obligated if something comes up. It was good to have the moral support this first run, but I can tackle some of these salons alone."

"We'll take it week by week," Jeremy said. "Besides, I'm invested in this now, too. I have to admit, when we first started out, I was skeptical. All the evidence that you had indicating Bella could be alive was circumstantial. But now we've found two people who clearly knew her from *Castleton*. Everything is pointing toward Bella being alive, and I want to help figure out what happened in any way I can."

"Thanks, Jeremy. I guess today was a productive day. One more person inadvertently confirmed that my sister is alive. That's huge."

Jeremy dropped Anna off at her house. Since it was still early in the evening, she walked over to *Bella's Dream* to check on the shop before returning home.

Anna sat by the picture window in her living room, sipping a mug of lavender tea and watching the sun go down behind the oak trees that lined her street.

She smiled when she saw Casper sitting in front of her gate and meowing. She went out to open the door. The orange cat was a sight for sore eyes.

Did Casper miss her because she hadn't been at the shop as much this week, or was he just looking for extra meals to fatten up for the winter? It was hard to tell with that little guy.

Anna scooped some canned chicken onto a paper plate and placed it on the front porch. She took her tea outside to keep him company while he ate. If Casper kept coming to her home instead of going to *Bella's Dream*, she would need to get him a dish for her house, in addition to the one she had at the shop. Anna laughed at herself. For someone who didn't own a cat, she sure had a lot of things for Casper.

While Casper ate, Anna pulled the list of salons from her pocket.

"There are still twenty left to visit," she found herself saying to Casper. His ears pointed forward in Anna's direction. She took that as a sign that he was listening while he ate.

"If I wait until Jeremy is free on Monday, it will take five weeks to get through the list. And there are no guarantees that I'll have any more useful information when I'm finished. It's possible that Bella relocated to an entirely different part of the state. I need to plow through this list as quickly as possible, so that I'll either find Bella sooner, or I can begin to implement a new plan."

Casper finished eating and jumped up onto Anna's lap. She pulled back her mug of tea so he wouldn't knock it over. Casper curled up on her lap while she petted him and continued her line of thinking.

"Visiting these salons could be mostly busy work. I don't need anyone for that. I'm going to go when I can and get through some of these salons on my own rather than waiting for Jeremy next Monday."

She felt better to have made this decision, and her mood immediately improved.

After spending more time than usual with Anna, Casper hopped off her lap and waited by the front gate. She laughed as she opened the gate. "You're such a gentleman, Casper."

Anna spent the rest of the evening reading on her couch, then went to bed early.

While she was on her way to *Bella's Dream* on Tuesday morning, Allie called.

"Hi, Anna. We're going to visit Aunt Violet this afternoon after lunch. Are you still able to come with us so you can ask her your questions?"

"I'd love to. Can I meet you at your house, though? It might be awkward for me to show up alone."

Allie chuckled. "Sure, that makes sense. Can you come to our house at 1:30?"

"That works for me. I'll see you then."

Anna left *Bella's Dream* at 12:30, since foot traffic was slow, and stopped at a sandwich shop for lunch.

When she arrived at Allie's and Jackson's house, they came out.

"Let's take our car," Jackson suggested.

She hopped into the backseat. "Thanks for the ride."

"Charlie called a few minutes ago," Jackson said, as he backed out of the driveway. "The lab confirmed that the hot fudge in the jar you found behind the spice rack was indeed laced with arsenic and strychnine. So was the top layer of fudge on Chester's sundae. The rest of the fudge was fine."

"Poor Uncle Chester didn't stand a chance," Allie said.

Jackson pulled into the driveway of a large black and white house with a wraparound porch. It seemed to Anna to be more the size of a small inn than a home. Violet had tea and pastries on the table in the formal dining room.

"People have been bringing me all sorts of food and snacks since Chester died," Violet said. "Please, you must help me eat some of these, or I won't be able to fit through the door."

Anna took a piece of cinnamon cake to enjoy with her coffee.

"Dear, I'm so sorry you had to be present for that awful event on Saturday," Violet said, shaking her head. "What a day."

"It was terrible. I'm just sorry that whoever did this used my hot fudge sundae bar as a pretense for such a horrible crime."

"Oh, please don't feel that way. I'm sure there was nothing you could have done to stop what happened. I don't blame you at all. Chester had his share of enemies, and I'm sure whoever did this would have found another way, even if you hadn't hosted the hot fudge sundae bar."

Violet helped herself to a second piece of cake, then showed Allie some clothes and a painting she had bought on Sunday morning.

Allie was right. Violet certainly wasn't conducting herself like a wife in mourning. The question was, did that make her a killer?

CHAPTER 8

"**You're** probably right," Anna said to Violet, trying to steer the conversation back to Chester's death. "The killer would likely have found a way to get to Chester, even without the party. But he or she *did* choose my sundae bar as their opportunity for murder. I'd like to get to the bottom of who did that."

"Oh. Don't you think you should leave the matter to the police?"

If Anna wasn't mistaken, Violet's tone betrayed her annoyance.

"Detective Doyle will sort it all out. There's no point in wasting your time and energy. That's what we pay taxes for, isn't it? Let's let the professionals handle it."

"I suppose that's true, Aunt Violet," Allie said. "But still, it's a terrible thing that happened to Uncle Chester, and it was right in our own home. We are grateful to Anna for looking into this. Would you be able to answer a few of her questions?"

Violet hesitated before agreeing. "Okay, dear. For you and Jackson. What would you like to know, Anna?"

"You probably knew Chester better than anyone. Do you have any idea who could have done this?" Anna asked. "It had to be someone who was at the party. Nobody could have snuck in and poisoned Chester's sundae without being seen."

"Hmm, I suppose you're right. I can think of many people who carried one type of grudge or another against him, but the person would have had to have been at the party. And many of the people at the party barely knew Chester."

"Among those who were present, who would you say had the biggest motive?" Allie asked.

"Oh, I hate to throw stones. I wouldn't want to cause problems for anyone. Why don't we just try to forget about it and move on?" Violet said. "All this talk of murder is really beginning to depress me."

Anna glanced over at Allie and Jackson, who appeared to be equally as frustrated with Violet's attitude.

"Aunt Violet, I know this is difficult, but please tell us what you think," Allie insisted.

"Well, if I must, I'd say Drake held the biggest grudge against Chester. But I don't think he'd do something so extreme. You know, we may have to resolve ourselves to the fact that we may never know who did this."

Allie ignored Violet's last comment. "Is there another reason you think Drake might have done it, besides his bitterness toward Uncle Chester?"

Violet took a deep breath. "Do you remember how he came in wearing that... what did he call it? Oh, yes, a man bag. It was quite a handsome leather bag, but I've never seen him carry one before.

Don't you think it's quite a coincidence that he brought that bag on the same day Chester was killed? If he had been carrying a jar of hot fudge in that bag, nobody would have noticed."

"That's a good point," Allie said. "I forgot about that. Anna, you wouldn't have seen the bag, because by the time you arrived, Drake had put it in the coat closet. He carried it with him for a little while before putting it away. He could easily have slipped into the kitchen and unloaded the jar of fudge before putting it in the closet."

"Oh, I do hope it wasn't Drake. I adore that young man," Violet said. "He has always been so kind to me."

"What were you doing when the sundaes were being served?" Anna asked. "Allie and Jackson were standing at the front of the room, and they didn't notice anything unusual. Did *you* happen to see anything suspicious?"

"Chester and I were the first to get our sundaes. After that, we chatted with some of the other guests."

"Were you in the living room the whole time?" Anna asked.

"Oh, I don't really recall. Chester and I were chatting with some guests. I did go to the restroom at one point, but I was in the living room for most of the time. I didn't notice anything unusual, either."

If Violet went to the restroom, that means that some of her time was unaccounted for. Violet could have slipped into the kitchen.

"We understand that Chester went into the kitchen for a cup of water," Anna said.

"Yes, the police told me that that's where they think it happened. I couldn't tell you that. By the time I came out of the bathroom, Chester was in the living room. I didn't even know he left."

"What about Eliza?" Anna asked. "Someone mentioned to us that she wanted to quit working for Chester but that he wouldn't let her."

"I'll bet it was Nick who told you that. Well, I can't deny that it's true. But Eliza has been saying she wants to leave for years. That's not anything new. Besides, Chester paid her better than any other job would have paid her. In fact, he recently gave her a raise. I don't believe she really wanted to leave. And if she did, she wouldn't have killed Chester over it."

"Is there anyone you *do* believe would have killed him?" Anna asked.

"I can't say that there is." She shrugged her shoulders. "It's all a mystery to me. That's why I think we should let the police sort it out and get on with our lives. I don't want to go around accusing my family and friends."

Violet directed the conversation toward other topics, and by the end of their visit, it felt more like a social call than anything else. After about an hour, Allie and Jackson drove Anna back to their house, where she had left her car.

"Violet doesn't seem too distressed about losing her husband," Anna noted. "And she didn't seem all that concerned with learning who killed him."

"I'd have to agree," Jackson said. "I noticed that yesterday, but I was still trying to give her the benefit of the doubt. I mean, it must have been extremely difficult to live with Chester, and if I'm being honest, I'm not surprised that she might feel somewhat relieved to be free. But the man isn't even in the ground yet."

"I know," Allie said. "I hate to say it, but if she cares so little, maybe it *was* Aunt Violet who killed Uncle Chester."

"She did say that she went to the restroom after getting

her ice cream," Anna said. "She could be lying. Maybe she was waiting for her chance and slipped into the kitchen instead."

"I was thinking the same thing," Jackson said.

"What bothers me the most is that she seemed to be trying to discourage us from asking questions," Anna said. "You would think she would *want* answers. Unfortunately, we need to keep her on the short list of suspects."

"I think Drake stays on there, too," Jackson said. "If he was carrying a bag, and he didn't usually do that, it could have been for the purpose of hiding the jar of poisoned hot fudge."

"The next person I'd like to talk with is Nick," Anna said. "We need to find out where he was when Chester was in the kitchen. If he didn't do it, he might have some additional insight as to who did."

"Sure," Allie said. "Eliza and Dorothea are going to spend the evening with Violet, so Uncle Nick is coming over for dinner tonight. The family has been trying to get together as much as possible during this difficult time. We could bring him by the ice cream shop afterwards for dessert."

"Perfect. I'll make sure I'm there tonight."

Anna hopped into her car and returned to *Bella's Dream*.

Joe had just arrived for his two scoops of ice cream.

"Maple walnut again?" Velma asked as he took his usual stool.

Joe removed his Red Sox cap and nodded.

After Velma served him his ice cream, Anna motioned for Joe to join her in a booth and gave him an update on her trip to Maine the previous day, including Carly's strange behavior when Anna mentioned *Castleton*.

"That's the second time you got that reaction," Joe said.

Anna nodded. "Jeremy thinks it further confirms that Bella

did indeed take classes at *Castleton,* but that she made it clear that if anyone came asking about her, to pretend they didn't know her. I tend to agree."

"It certainly does appear that way."

"I'm thinking of hitting a few more schools on the list this week alone rather than waiting until Jeremy has another day off. I want to get through the list you gave me as soon as possible. But this time, we decided that I wouldn't mention *Castleton.* Instead, I'm going to say that I went to high school with Bella and am trying to track her down for an upcoming reunion."

"If you need some moral support, I'd be happy to take a ride with you," Joe said.

"I appreciate it, but I think I'm okay for now." Anna preferred to use Joe for the portions of the investigation that required more expertise. It was possible that she wouldn't learn anything, anyway.

When they finished talking, Joe took his usual seat at the counter to chat with the staff. Just after he left, Todd came in, taking the stool that Joe had just vacated.

"I was in the area, so I thought I'd check on you after Saturday. I was hoping to get back to town before now, but it's been hectic at work."

"It's nice of you to come by, especially after everything you did for me on Saturday."

"I wanted to make sure you were okay," Todd said. "I mean, we *did* see a man get murdered."

"Thank you. I just want to know who used my hot fudge sundae bar to commit murder."

"The police will figure that out."

Anna ordered a hot fudge sundae for Todd. "At least let me

make good on that promise for a sundae, which you never got on Saturday."

"That's an offer I can't turn down," Todd said.

"Would you like to go into the dining room?" Anna asked. "While you're here, I might as well take the opportunity to run a few things by you."

"Sure," he said, following her to the booth that she and Joe had been sitting in.

"I went with Allie and Jackson this afternoon to talk with Violet. She was extremely nonchalant about what happened. She didn't look like a woman in mourning at all. The same was true for Drake when we talked with him yesterday. Allie and Drake are coming here with Nick after dinner tonight. I'm hoping to get some more information."

Todd put down his spoon and stared wide-eyed at Anna. "Wait, you're questioning suspects?"

"As I said, I need to know who did this. I've helped the police solve a few crimes since I moved to Seagull Cove. I seem to have a knack for it."

"Impressive," he said. "Do you have a theory yet?"

"I'm just gathering information for now. It's tough, because Chester had a lot of enemies."

Todd was silent for moment. "Would you mind if I stuck around while you talk to Nick?"

"I don't see why not," Anna said, surprised at his interest. "But I don't know what time they're coming. Don't you have to get back to work?"

"My laptop is in my car. I could do some work in here if I won't be bothering anyone."

"Of course not. Actually, it might be a good idea, since you were at the party. Maybe you'll be able to pick up on something that I missed."

"I doubt that, but I'd like to help."

Anna filled Todd in on Violet's strange behavior, Drake's man bag, and Drake's and Nick's theory that Eliza did it because Chester wouldn't let her quit her job. "Now that you're up to speed, I'll leave you to get some work done."

CHAPTER 9

A couple of hours later, Allie and Jackson arrived at *Bella's Dream* with Nick. They each ordered a dish of ice cream and brought it into the dining room.

Shortly after, Anna and Todd joined them.

Allie scooted over to make room for Anna, and Todd dragged a chair to the head of the table so the others wouldn't be too crowded.

"We still can't believe what happened to Chester," Anna said. "It seems like a bad dream."

Nick took a generous spoonful of ice cream. "This is delicious. What flavor is it, maple walnut?"

"Um, yes, I just started carrying it this fall. Again, we are sorry for your loss. I can't imagine what you must be going through."

"Oh, yes. Chester. We're just devastated," Nick said.

Anna glanced over at Todd, who was studying Nick. She guessed that his expression of grief rang as hollow to Todd's ears as it did to Anna's.

"Now that you've had a few days to think about it, do you

have any more thoughts on who might have done this to your brother?" Anna asked.

A smile crept its way on to Nick's lips. "My brother sure knew how to rub folks the wrong way. And he did seem to be even moodier lately than he usually was. Don't you think so?" he asked, looking at Allie and Jackson.

"I have to say, Nick is right. I remember noticing that on a couple of occasions," Jackson said.

"Drake noticed it, too," Nick said. "But as cranky as Chester could be, I never thought he would have done something so drastic as to elicit that type of response. Murder takes it to a whole new level."

"So, are you saying that you believe that the motive was revenge, but that you just don't know for what?" Todd asked.

Nick took another spoonful of ice cream while he looked at Todd thoughtfully. "Knowing Chester, I'd say that's a pretty safe assumption. He had a way of ignoring how his words and actions would affect other people. He did and said whatever he felt like. I don't know how Violet put up with him all these years. Or Eliza, for that matter."

"You've probably known Chester longer than anyone," Anna said.

Nick thought for a moment. "Yes, I guess it's fair to say that. He's my younger brother, so I knew him since the day he was born. Our parents have passed, as well as our sister, so I guess I'm the only one left in this world who could say they knew Chester his whole life."

"Is there anyone, besides Eliza, who stands out in your mind as having a particularly strong motive for murder?"

Nick took another bite of ice cream and looked at them

over his spoon with narrowed eyes. "Why so many questions? You sound like police officers."

Anna leaned back in her seat. "Well, I guess this murder just feels personal. We were all there when he died, and the killer *did* use my sundae bar as a pretext to commit murder. I'd like to know what happened."

"We feel the same way," Jackson added. "It's hard to think of anything else except what happened on Saturday. What was supposed to be a joyful celebration of our first anniversary turned tragic. We feel like we have a personal stake in this too, even beyond the fact that Uncle Chester was a relative."

Nick appeared to contemplate their predicament. "Yes, the circumstances were unfortunate. I can see how you'd feel that way. But try not to take it personally. Chester had a lot of enemies, and your party was probably just a convenient place to do it."

It didn't sound like Nick had thought this through.

"That is true. But there were only twenty-three guests at the party," Anna said. "Since the killer wouldn't have been able to enter the house undetected, it stands to reason that whoever did this had to be someone on the guest list."

"And since my family and our friends barely knew Chester, I think it's safe to say that it was a member of Allie's family or one of the two close family friends who was present," Jackson said.

"You're referring to Dorothea and Eliza," Nick said. "Hmm, I suppose you're right. That does narrow the pool of suspects considerably."

Todd continued to look intently between Nick and Anna.

"If you look at it that way, that means it would have to be

Drake, Violet, Eliza, Dorothea, Allie, Jackson, or myself," Nick continued.

"Actually, Allie and Jackson were standing next to me greeting guests as they came to the sundae bar, so it couldn't have been either of them."

"Oh, right. I remember that." Nick chuckled. "Not that I ever thought the two of you would be capable of such a thing."

"Uncle Chester was the first guest to get his sundae," Allie said.

Nick shook his head. "Figures. He always had to be first for everything."

"At some point, Chester went into the kitchen to get some water," Anna said. "That is where his sundae was likely poisoned. Violet says she left to go to the restroom, so she didn't see him go in the kitchen."

"I see," Nick said.

"Unfortunately, we don't know what happened after that. We don't know if the killer was already in the kitchen, or if he or she followed Chester," Anna said. "I'm guessing that, since the jar of poisoned fudge was found hidden behind the spice rack, that someone quickly dumped the fudge into his sundae while Chester was getting his water from the cooler in the butler's pantry, and then stashed it behind the spices."

"Makes sense," Nick said.

"Did you happen to notice anyone go into the kitchen around that time?" Anna asked.

Nick stared into his ice cream. "It's hard to remember. I was milling about, talking to just about everyone. I wasn't really looking in the direction of the kitchen."

"Do you remember Violet going to the restroom?" Anna asked.

Nick shook his head. "No. But that doesn't mean she didn't. Sorry that I'm not much help. I tend to be a social butterfly, and I really wasn't paying attention to Chester. To be honest, I was happy to avoid him. As we said, he had been quite moody."

"What about Dorothea?" Anna asked. "Did she have a motive to kill Chester?"

Nick smirked. "You'd have to ask Dorothea about that."

"What do you mean by that, Uncle Nick?" Allie asked.

"I have my suspicions about what her motive could be, but it's better that you ask Dorothea. They are only suspicions."

"Can you at least give us a hint, so we know what we're asking about?" Jackson asked.

"Ask her about her recent financial investments," Nick said. "She recently lost a lot of money through Chester's advice. Chester was hitting up everyone he knew for investment capital. He was planning to build a hotel by the beach, and he purchased a large plot of land. However, he didn't get the permits to implement his plan, so now they are all part owners of an unbuildable plot of land."

"I heard about that," Jackson said. "I was surprised. Chester was a shrewd businessman, and you could usually trust his investments. But he really blew this last one. Allie and I thought about investing some of our savings, but I'm glad we didn't."

"If you ask me, Chester was up to something sinister with that investment," Nick said.

"What do you mean?" Todd asked.

"I don't know, exactly," Nick said. "But Jackson is right about Chester being shrewd. There's no way he made a mistake that colossal. He was up to something. I guess we'll never know."

"You think it was some sort of scam?" Anna asked.

Nick shrugged his shoulders. "I don't have any proof, but my brother was too smart to buy a plot of land without knowing whether or not it was buildable." Nick took a paper napkin from the stainless-steel dispenser and wiped his mouth. Then he threw it into his empty dish and looked at Allie as if he were ready to leave.

Taking their cue from Nick, Allie and Jackson took their last bites of ice cream, and the three of them left the shop.

"I'll call you tonight," Allie whispered to Anna as she stood up.

Anna and Todd sat back down in the booth. "Well, that was impressive," Todd said. "You interviewed Nick like a pro."

"I guess you could say that sleuthing has become an unintended hobby."

Todd's eyes widened again. "I remember you saying that you had been involved in an investigation in the past, but I underestimated you. I thought maybe you offered a few opinions. But you're a regular amateur detective."

Anna laughed at Todd's surprised expression. "Believe it or not, being an amateur sleuth seems to run in my family," Anna said.

"Did your sister also have a knack for solving crimes?" Todd asked.

"No. My cousin Connie, who lives in Florida. It all started when I went to Florida for her wedding last November."

"Who'd have known that sort of thing could be hereditary?" Todd mused. "If you plan to continue investigating, I'd happy to lend you a hand. I feel like it's only right, since I was there when it happened."

"Do you mean it?"

"Of course."

"I would like that. I have a feeling Allie and Jackson would rather not be directly involved. Allie mentioned that she is uncomfortable asking family and friends whether they killed her uncle, which is completely understandable. I think they would appreciate it if I had someone else helping me out. I wouldn't want to do it alone."

"I'm happy to help. Are you going to talk to Dorothea next?"

"I think so. Allie told me she'd call me tonight, so once I talk to her, I'll find out the best way to go about doing that."

"Sounds good. I should go, but will you call me when you know your next step?" Todd asked.

"Absolutely. And thank you."

"Consider me your official sidekick for this case," Todd said with a smile. He pulled out his cell phone. "We should exchange phone numbers so you can call or text when you hear back from Allie."

Anna rattled off her digits, and Todd called her, so she'd have his number in her phone. Then she took her phone from her pocket and saved his contact information.

Just as she saved Todd's number, Anna looked up and found Jeremy sitting at the ice cream counter and looking in her direction. He quickly averted his gaze when Anna made eye contact. For some reason, she felt a twinge of guilt when she saw him, even though she had nothing to feel guilty about. She and Todd were not dating, and even if they were, she wasn't dating Jeremy, either. But she couldn't shake the feeling that she had hurt his feelings.

Anna walked Todd to the door, then went over to say hello to Jeremy.

"I was in the neighborhood, so I thought I'd stop in to say hello. I didn't mean to pull you away from anything important."

"Todd and I were just discussing the murder at Allie's and Jackson's anniversary party. Todd helped me with the sundae bar that afternoon, so he was there when it happened."

"Is he working for you now?" Jeremy asked, confused.

Anna laughed. "No. One of my employees came down with the flu and called in sick at the last minute. Todd happened to be here and offered to help for the afternoon."

"I see. That was nice of him."

Anna wasn't convinced that Jeremy's compliment of Todd was sincere.

"Are we still on for Monday?" Jeremy asked. "I'm anxious to see if we have any luck with some of the other salons on Joe's list."

"Absolutely," Anna said. "I'm anxious to get back to it, as well. In fact, I was considering going before then by myself if I can break away from work. I figured that since there are so many salons on the list, if we only go on Mondays, it will take us a while to get through the list."

"You're probably right," he said. "As much as I feel invested, I understand your impatience. But call if you go. I'll be dying of curiosity."

"I promise," Anna said. "You'll be the first to know what happens."

CHAPTER 10

*B*y the time Allie called Anna that evening, Anna had already closed up shop, fed Casper, and was on her way home.

"I hope it's not too late to call," Allie said.

"Not at all. I'm walking home from work."

"Uncle Nick stayed later than we expected. Drake ended up stopping by, so Uncle Nick stuck around for a little while longer. I don't mean to repeat myself, but I'm very disappointed in their behavior, especially Uncle Nick's this afternoon. Uncle Nick, Aunt Violet, and Drake all seem so unaffected by what happened. Uncle Nick and Drake asked me to try to get you to stop investigating and to leave the matter to the police."

"Is that what you and Jackson want?" Anna asked.

"No, of course not. It just feels like we're missing a lot of pieces to this puzzle. It makes me think that one of them could be guilty, because they are taking things so casually and don't seem anxious to have this crime solved. I hate that I am having these thoughts about my family."

"Try to take it one step at time. I know you and Jackson are uncomfortable questioning family members and friends."

"It is a bit awkward, and I'm having a hard time remaining impartial. But the police don't seem to be making any progress, and I need to know what happened. I can't be wondering if anyone in my family or among our friends is a killer." Allie paused. "Or I should say, I don't want to be wondering *who* is a killer. As Jackson keeps reminding me, someone obviously did it."

"In that case, I have some news that might lift your spirits. Todd offered to help me," Anna said. "So, you don't have to accompany me anymore when I talk to people. You can just help direct us behind the scenes."

"That is wonderful news," Allie said. "Please thank Todd for me."

"I think we should talk to Dorothea next. Do you know the best way for Todd and me to reach her?"

"Dorothea lives in Seagull Cove. In fact, she walks Mile Long Beach every morning as the sun is rising. You could easily find her there."

That would be early for Todd to get to Seagull Cove, but Anna could talk to her alone if need be. Even if she was the killer, there would be plenty of people around.

"That's perfect," Anna said. "I'll go down to the beach tomorrow morning and see if I can pretend to run into her."

"Good luck," Allie said. "Promise me that you'll keep us posted every step of the way."

"I promise." Anna glanced at the time on her phone as she ended the call with Allie. It was after 9:30. She didn't want to call Todd this late. She would just have to talk to Dorothea alone the following morning.

As she was unlocking her front door, her phone pinged with a text from Todd.

Did you talk to Allie?

Instead of texting him back, she called him. "Hi, Todd. I just finished talking to her. I was afraid it might be too late to call, so I was going to touch base with you tomorrow."

"Don't worry about that. I'm a night owl, so it's rarely too late to call."

"In that case, you're not going to like this plan." She relayed her conversation with Allie and her plans to 'run into' Dorothea the following morning on the beach.

"Ouch. That's early, but I'll be there. I'll meet you at the beginning of the beach, the side closest to the cove, at 7:00."

"Are you sure?" Anna asked.

"Gloucester isn't too far away. I can manage."

"Okay. I'll see you then."

Anna called it an early night because of her newly made morning plans and set her alarm for 6:00. She hadn't been up that early for a while.

Anna hit the snooze button a couple of times before getting up. When it rang for the third time, she dragged herself out of bed.

Anna decided to gulp a quick cup of coffee and a yogurt, so her mind would be reasonably sharp when she talked to Dorothea before she drove to Mile Long Beach. Todd was waiting in his BMW, right where he promised to be.

"Hi, Todd. Thanks for coming out so early."

"I have to admit, it was painful. But I'm looking forward to seeing my favorite amateur detective in action."

"Do you know a lot of *other* detectives?" Anna asked sarcastically.

He shrugged his shoulders and smiled playfully. "I guess not. But I have a feeling you'd still be my favorite."

The two began walking along the sidewalk that ran parallel to the beach. The sun had just risen over the water, leaving the sky a dusty orange. There were a fair amount of people walking the beach, mostly young adults, who Anna guessed were getting in their exercise before work.

After walking about a quarter of a mile, Anna spotted a woman up ahead who looked like Dorothea. Her dark hair was fixed firmly in place with hairspray, barely moving from the breeze coming off the ocean.

Anna pointed to the woman. "I think that's her."

Anna and Todd picked up their pace until they were walking beside the woman.

"It's Dorothea, isn't it?" Anna asked, even though she knew by now that it was her.

"Yes. I'm sorry, do I know you?" Dorothea asked. She appeared to be searching her memory.

"It's Anna and Todd from the anniversary party on Saturday," Anna said.

"Oh, yes. Forgive me. You two ran the ice cream sundae bar, right?"

"That's us," Todd said.

"It's a beautiful morning for a walk," Anna said. It was warm enough to be out without a jacket but cool enough so as not to be hot while walking.

"Autumn is one of my favorite seasons for that exact reason."

"We're very sorry for the loss of your friend," Anna said. "Allie tells me that you are a close friend of the family."

"That's true. I've known Allie since she was born, and I

knew her mother long before that. I grew up on the same street as Joy, Nick, and Chester, right here in Seagull Cove. Back then, I didn't know Chester nearly as well as I knew Joy, mind you. Chester was a few years younger."

"Todd and I were just talking about what happened. It's hard to imagine that someone would poison a man's hot fudge sundae."

"You obviously didn't know Chester," Dorothea said.

"We did hear that he tended to rub folks the wrong way," Todd chimed in.

Dorothea laughed dramatically. "That's an understatement! That man had a knack for getting under people's skin."

"Getting under people's skin is one thing," Anna said. "Getting poisoned to death takes it to quite another level."

"I suppose you're right. But if I had to pick from anyone I know, I'm the least surprised that Chester met that type of death. I hate to speak ill of the dead, but Violet is better off without him."

Anna felt her jaw drop at Dorothea's statement, and Dorothea quickly took back her comment.

"I'm sorry. I shouldn't have said that."

"We heard something about a financial investment of Chester's that caused many people to lose money," Todd said.

"Oh, I see you've been talking to Nick. You couldn't exactly call that an investment. Don't tell me he thinks I killed Chester over that."

"He didn't say that," Anna said, even though he kind of did.

"Nick is quick to point the finger, which, in my book, means that it was likely Nick or Drake. They both stood to gain financially from Chester's death. Of course, Violet would get the most amount of money from his estate, but I happen to know that Nick, as well as Drake, Allie, and Oliver are also in the will. Of course, Allie would never dream of doing such a thing to Chester. For some strange reason, she loved the man. Probably because her mother did."

"Do you know who else lost money in the investment?" Anna asked.

"I know there were others, but I don't know who they were. I may have lost a good chunk of my retirement, but what good would it do for me to kill Chester over it?" She shook her head. "As much of a jerk as he could be, Chester was usually a shrewd investor. That's why I took him at his word without doing as much research as I should have. He told me it was a fool-proof investment, but it turned out I was the fool."

"Does Violet know about this?" Anna asked.

"Of course. Chester lost money, too. Not as much as I did, mind you. He was planning on using more of his own funds in the construction of the building. If you ask me, he asked his friends to invest in the land, the riskiest part, in case it fell through. There's no way a man like Chester didn't know the risk he was taking with our money."

"Did Chester give an explanation of what went wrong?" Todd asked.

"No. But Violet had the strangest reaction when I told her about it a few weeks ago. She didn't seem surprised at all. She told me to let it go for now, and that she'd make it right later."

"Did she say what she meant by that?" Anna asked.

Dorothea shook her head. Then her eyes flew open. "You don't suppose she was planning to kill Chester all along, do you?"

The thought *had* crossed Anna's mind. "It's possible. The

77

thing that doesn't make sense to me about that theory, though, is that we heard from more than one person that Violet had been doting over Chester lately. Her family says that she had more patience with him than ever. That doesn't sound like a woman who was planning to kill her husband. Unless, of course, she was trying to throw attention off herself."

"That's true. She would defend his behavior a lot recently, and she was doing more for him than ever before. She wouldn't even come out with Eliza and me to our monthly dinner. She insisted on staying home to cook for Chester."

"I would think if she were planning to kill him, she'd want to avoid him," Todd said.

"Come to think of it, her behavior didn't make a lot of sense. When she told me not to worry about the investment, I was angry. At first, I thought she was trying to brush me off. I almost didn't come to the party, but I didn't want to disappoint Allie and Jackson, so I went. I still can't understand why she was making excuses for Chester's behavior."

Dorothea glanced at her watch. "Well, I really must be going. That's my car." She pointed to an old black Mercedes. "You should really talk to Eliza if you want to know more about who was involved in the investment. She's still working at Chester's office. Violet asked her to stay on for a couple of weeks to close out his business affairs."

"We'll do that," Anna said. "I just have one more question. We think that the killer poisoned Chester's sundae in the kitchen. Did you happen to see anyone go into the kitchen shortly after the sundae bar opened?"

"I don't think so. At least not that I remember."

Anna and Todd thanked Dorothea for her time and walked back toward their cars.

"I'm sorry you came over to Seagull Cove for nothing," Anna said as they changed directions and walked back toward their cars.

"Are you kidding? I got to experience a window into the mind of Anna McBride," Todd said. "Besides, it feels good to be up and out this early, and to have already had my morning exercise. I should do it more often."

Anna glanced at Todd's biceps. He obviously did more to stay in shape than just a morning walk.

"I have to meet a client in Gloucester in an hour, but would you like to meet tomorrow morning to talk to Eliza? My first client isn't until the afternoon."

"That would be great. I'll get the address from Allie."

"Perfect," Todd said. "Text me your address, and I'll pick you up at 9:00."

CHAPTER 11

*A*fter her walk with Todd and their conversation with Dorothea, Anna returned home to shower and change. Then she headed to Main Street early to get some breakfast at *Cove Coffee*.

On her way down the front walkway, Anna turned to admire Wanda's front porch. The density of potted yellow, orange, and purple mums, red valerian, sunflowers, and an array of other muted colors made it look more like a garden than a porch. Then she glanced at her own porch. Anna needed to up her game.

Autumn had come quickly, and she never got out to buy fall flowers. At this point, there was no use spending money on plants that wouldn't last outside much longer. The first frost of the season could come any night now. Oh, well. There was always next year.

Anna bought a breakfast sandwich and a large hazelnut coffee at *Cove Coffee* and found a seat by a window.

Sonja smiled when she spotted Anna. "Do you mind if I join you for a few minutes?"

"I was hoping you might," Anna said. "It's so much easier to get a table this time of year than it was over the summer. I miss the business, but I don't miss the lines at all the Main Street shops."

"The fall is always a nice change of pace around here. We'll still get some tourists through the next couple of weeks, while the foliage is in bloom, but the pace is much slower than the summer. Foot traffic will slow down for November, but after Thanksgiving, we'll get a few more busy weeks, thanks to Seagull Cove's Christmas festivities."

"Have you seen Ruthie or Rosie lately?" Anna asked.

"I haven't seen Rosie," Sonja said. "The inn is always booked solid with leaf peepers through October. But Ruthie came in earlier this week. She is busy compiling her book of poetry."

"That's great news," Anna said. "I hope she completes it in time for the holidays."

"That's what Ruthie is aiming for. She included a few Christmas and winter selections. She's excited about the cover design. Her designer just completed the final draft. If you stop by, I'm sure you can convince her to show you."

"I'll do that. I'll blast it out on my social media sites, as well, to help her drum up some pre-release excitement."

"Great idea," Sonja said.

Anna finished her breakfast at *Cove Coffee*, then went to *Bella's Dream*. Soon Velma and Mary arrived for their shift.

"Did I see you walking the beach with Todd Devonshire this morning?" Velma asked before she even said hello.

Oh, boy. It figures that Velma saw her. She would never let Anna live that one down.

"Since Todd was helping me with the hot fudge sundae bar

when Chester was killed on Saturday, we've teamed up to do some investigating."

"I'm telling you, Anna, that man is into you. First, he makes it a point to come in here regularly, ever since you took over the shop. Then he offers to help you run a hot fudge sundae bar at a party on a Saturday afternoon. And now, he's your sidekick for this investigation. The man is just looking for excuses to spend time with you."

"Is he cute?" Mary asked.

"Is he ever!" Velma said dreamily, leaning on the counter. "And rich."

Mary scrunched up her nose. "Rich is overrated. I vote for Jeremy."

Anna laughed and shook her head. "You two *do* realize that I'm not dating either of them, don't you?"

Velma winked at Mary. "She doesn't *think* she is."

Mary chuckled.

"I definitely am *not*. I outright told Jeremy that I wasn't looking for a relationship, and the conversation has never even come up with Todd."

Although, she did think she saw disappointment on Jeremy's face when he saw her and Todd exchanging phone numbers. Even though it was just for the case, and not because of any personal relationship.

"Well, if I had those two men vying for my attention, I wouldn't waste any time choosing between them," Mary said. "Then again, maybe I'd take my time deciding. How many times does a woman have two handsome gentlemen interested in dating her?"

Anna was about to protest that Todd had never expressed interest and Jeremy had, but it was months ago, and she told him she wasn't interested in a relationship. But she knew it would be a losing battle, so she swallowed her response.

"Leave it to you to have your first hot fudge sundae bar end in murder," Velma said.

"You do seem to have a knack for getting entangled in criminal investigations," Mary said.

Anna was grateful for the change in topic. And she couldn't argue with that. Not to mention her investigation into Bella's alleged death. But she wasn't going to bring that up.

"Speaking of Chester, have you made any progress?" Velma asked.

"Not as much as I'd like. We narrowed it down to five people who were both present at Allie's and Jackson's party, and who knew Chester well enough to have a motive to kill him."

"You mean, there were five people at that party who had a motive?" Velma asked.

"All of Seagull Cove seems to have a motive. But only those at the party would have had the opportunity to do it. Someone brought in a jar of hot fudge that was laced with poison, and when nobody was looking, they poured the fudge onto Chester's hot fudge sundae."

"And nobody saw anyone do that?" Mary asked.

"Apparently not," Anna said. "We think it was done when Chester went into the kitchen, but nobody seems to have been paying attention to who was with him at the time. It's very frustrating. Todd and I have one last person to interview tomorrow, but so far, it could have been any of them. I hope Charlie is making more progress than we are."

Anna spent the whole day at *Bella's Dream*, mostly chatting with customers and staff, since her employees could easily handle the foot traffic.

When it was time to close up shop, Anna kept Casper company on the back stoop while he ate. Then she walked home. She plopped onto her couch and called Allie to update her on their conversation with Dorothea earlier that morning.

"Dorothea is right. It wasn't like Uncle Chester to make such a bad business mistake. I can't imagine he would take such a risk with his investors' money. It's not good business practice, and Uncle Chester was an investment wiz."

"Dorothea told us that Eliza is still working at Chester's office to close out his affairs, so Todd and I were planning to pop in tomorrow to talk with her. Could you send me Chester's office address?"

"I'm texting it right now. Let me know how it goes."

After she hung up with Allie, Anna shot Todd a text confirming their plans for the following morning and sent him her home address, since he had insisted on picking her up.

With those tasks done, Anna's stomach reminded her that she hadn't eaten much for dinner. She baked half of an acorn squash, which she had picked up at the farmstand with Jeremy, then added some butter, brown sugar, and cinnamon, and spent a quiet evening reading on her couch.

The following morning, Todd picked Anna up at 9:00 as promised, and they were off to Chester's office to talk to Eliza.

The GPS brought them to a grey and white low-rise office building near the highway. They climbed a flight of stairs to the second floor and found the office number that Allie had texted to Anna. The glass door, which was propped open with a rubber doorstop, led to a large office suite. Eliza sat at the reception desk in the otherwise empty suite tapping away on her computer.

She looked up when Anna and Todd entered and studied their faces, as if trying to place them. Then, she appeared to give up. "How can I help you?"

"Hi, Eliza. I'm Anna, and this is Todd. We ran the hot fudge sundae bar at Allie's and Jackson's anniversary party last weekend."

Recognition spread across her face. "Oh, yes, of course."

"We're so sorry for your loss. We were told that you are still working here, and we were hoping to ask you a few questions."

"Questions about what?" Eliza asked.

"About Chester. Allie and Jackson are obviously very shaken up over what happened, so we promised to help figure out who did this."

"We know how busy you must be, so we won't take up too much of your time," Todd added.

"Those poor kids. Sure, I suppose I could answer a few questions. Just let me save this letter." She clicked on the computer's mouse, then turned her attention back to Anna and Todd. "I'll be here until the end of next week. I promised Violet that I'd help her close out Chester's investments and inform his business associates of his death. It's the least I can do for her." Eliza stood and motioned for them to sit on a small couch in the waiting area, and she sat on a chair facing them.

"I can only spare a few minutes. I have a lot of work to do."

"Okay, then. We'll get right down to it," Anna said. "Being Chester's secretary, you spent a lot of time with him. Is there anyone who stands out in your mind as a strong suspect?"

Eliza took a deep breath. "I don't know how to say this tactfully."

"Chester rubbed a lot of people the wrong way," Todd supplied.

Eliza gave them a half smile. "So, you've heard."

"It makes finding his killer a lot more difficult," Anna said.

"I would imagine so. It really could have been anybody. Violet doesn't seem to want to dwell on his death. She seems to be trying to move on, so we haven't talked much about it."

"She seems to want to move on before her husband is even buried," Anna said.

"It may seem cold, but if you had known Chester, you'd understand. He made her life difficult. Especially these past couple of months."

"We heard that. What was different about those months?" Anna asked.

"Something was bothering Chester, but I couldn't tell you what. He seemed off. He took more time off than I had ever seen him take, he was frequently distracted, and he was even more demanding of Violet than usual."

"And of you, too, I'm sure. It must have been hard to work for a man like that," Anna said.

"I can't deny that. But at least I could leave at 5:00 every day. Violet had to live with the man."

"Are you saying you think Violet could have killed him?"

Eliza looked at the floor. "I don't really know. I wouldn't have thought so, but we all know that it had to be someone at the party who knew Chester. That considerably narrows the pool of potential killers."

"That's what we're thinking, too," Todd said.

"As best as we can figure, the killer poisoned Chester's sundae when he went into the kitchen for a glass of water," Anna said.

Eliza didn't respond.

"Eliza, did you see something at the party?" Anna asked.

"I did. And it's been bothering me ever since Saturday. I was talking with Violet and Chester when Chester excused himself to go into the kitchen for a glass of water. I noticed that Violet was distracted all day, and she barely took her eyes off Chester during the whole time that we talked. When Chester went into the kitchen, she excused herself and followed him."

CHAPTER 12

*A*nna glanced at Todd, then back at Eliza, who was fidgeting with a pen.

Finally, they had encountered someone who saw Chester go into the kitchen. And apparently, Violet did, too.

"Are you sure?" Anna asked.

"Positive. I was watching out for Violet that day, because, as I said, Chester had been particularly short-tempered the previous day at work, and I was worried about her. Dorothea and I invited Violet out to dinner on Friday, but Violet insisted on staying home with Chester. I was surprised that she didn't jump at the chance to get out. I don't know how she was putting up with it. I tried talking to her about it before the party, but she pretended she didn't know what I was talking about. She minimized the situation, saying that Chester was just being Chester and that his behavior wasn't bothering her."

"We understand you wanted to quit your job, but that Chester wouldn't let you."

Eliza took a deep breath. "I won't deny that. Chester was a

difficult boss, as I'm sure you can imagine. I am grateful that he gave me a job when I needed it most, but he was still difficult to work for. I was ready to spread my wings. I began working for Chester fifteen years ago, after my husband passed away. At the time, I didn't have a lot of work experience, but Violet convinced Chester to give me a chance. Last month, when I told him that I had been offered another job and wanted to give my notice, Chester threatened to sabotage my job offer if I left. Since this is the only job that I've held in the past thirty years, and I had no other references, I didn't see much choice but to stay."

"Did you tell Violet about what happened?" Todd asked.

Eliza nodded. Then her eyes widened.

"What is it?" Anna asked.

"I just remembered something. When I told Violet what happened, she said that Chester's behavior wouldn't be a problem for much longer. She asked me to trust her and told me that I would understand later. I assumed that maybe he had been talking about retiring, but now... You don't suppose she was planning to kill him, do you?"

Anna recalled how Violet had said something similar to Dorothea when she told Violet about the money she lost in Chester's real estate investment. It wasn't looking good for Violet.

"It certainly does sound suspicious, under the circumstances. But I would hope that if things had grown that bad between them, she would just divorce him," Anna said.

"I would hope so, too," Todd said. "But maybe it was a question of the inheritance. People do crazy things not to have to give up the lifestyle they are accustomed to."

Eliza shook her head. "I don't think Violet is *that* attached

ANGELA K. RYAN

to her lifestyle. But if Chester was making it this difficult for me to leave my job, I've often wondered how difficult he would make it for Violet if she wanted to leave their marriage."

Violet was quickly moving to the top of Anna's list of suspects.

"Is there anyone else besides Violet you've noticed acting suspiciously lately?" Anna asked.

"There is one thing that happened recently that has me wondering," Eliza said. "I assume Dorothea told you about Chester's recent real estate investment disaster."

Anna and Todd nodded.

"Some people thought that Chester was purposefully careless with his investors' money, but I never believed that. As difficult as he could be in some ways, he took business seriously. I don't know what happened there, but I believe he made an honest mistake. He was on a bad streak. It wasn't the only bad investment he had made lately."

"So, what does this have to do with Chester's murder?" Anna asked.

"One morning I came into the office early and found Drake in Chester's office snapping pictures of some documents with his phone. I asked him what he was looking for, and he told me he was searching for information about Chester's latest scheme. The file he was taking pictures of had all the information on that real estate investment. Drake assured me that he wasn't looking to get Chester into trouble. He just wanted to know what his uncle was up to. I thought that was strange, so after he left, I looked at the file and figured out why he was so interested. His father was one of the investors who had lost his shirt when the building department denied Chester's request for a permit."

"Nick didn't tell us that he was one of the investors," Todd said.

"How did Drake react to seeing the files?" Anna asked.

"He seemed pleased to have found them. He didn't seem particularly angry, except that he did say that he didn't believe that his uncle would make a mistake like that by accident. He believed Chester was up to something sinister."

"Was there ever a confrontation between Drake and Chester?"

"Not that I know of. But that doesn't mean there wasn't."

"If Nick agreed with Drake and believed that Chester had been careless with his investment money, or worse, that Chester was conducting some sort of scam, he could have killed Chester out of revenge," Anna said.

"There was already a lot of bad blood between those two. Perhaps Drake saw something from those files that put him over the edge," Todd said.

The phone on Eliza's desk rang. "I have to get that. I'm waiting for someone to call me back."

Anna and Todd thanked Eliza for her time and left.

"What do you think?" Todd asked when they got back into Todd's BMW.

"Eliza did have a motive. If Chester wouldn't let Eliza leave to take another job, she could have killed him in order to gain her freedom," Anna said.

"Or it could be Nick," Todd added. "He conveniently forgot to mention that he was one of the investors in the real estate deal. It could even be Drake. Who knows how far Drake would go to protect his father and to get his inheritance early?"

"That's all true," Anna said. "But it's Violet's behavior that has me the most suspicious," Anna said.

"It *is* disturbing," Todd said. "Both Dorothea and Eliza told us that Violet outright said that Chester's behavior wouldn't be a problem for long."

"Eliza also said she saw Violet follow Chester into the kitchen, but if Eliza is the killer, she could be lying about that. However, if she was telling the truth, that gives Violet both motive *and* opportunity," Anna said.

"And despite Chester being more short-tempered lately and treating Violet worse, everyone says that Violet had been more patient with him than ever before," Todd added. "Maybe she had been planning to kill him all along and was being extra nice to him in front of others to throw suspicion off herself."

"We need to talk to Violet as soon as possible," Anna said.

"How are we going to arrange that?"

Anna pulled out her cell phone. "Let me see what Allie has to say."

After Anna relayed to Allie their conversation with Eliza, Allie agreed to meet Anna and Todd and take them to talk with Violet so they could confront her and get to the bottom of things.

"Are you sure you want to be present for that conversation, Allie?" Anna asked. "Todd and I could go alone."

"I want to come. Uncle Chester's services start tomorrow, and I don't want to have these unresolved questions in my mind about Aunt Violet."

"I'm sorry, Todd," Anna said, after disconnecting the

phone. "I shouldn't have assumed you had the time to come. I don't want to keep you from work."

"Are you kidding? It's like watching a soap opera unfold. I'd never get any work done wondering what's going to happen next, anyway."

Todd and Anna hopped back into Todd's car and drove back to Anna's house. Allie was already waiting for them in her car, which was parked in front of the white picket fence surrounding Anna's blue and white cottage. Todd motioned for Allie to join them, and she scooted into the backseat.

Within ten minutes, they were ringing Violet's doorbell. When Violet answered, she stood there with her mouth open, staring at the three of them.

CHAPTER 13

*V*iolet quickly composed herself. "Hello, there."

"Hi, Aunt Violet," Allie said. "I'm sorry to stop by unannounced, but there is something we really need to talk about."

Violet looked surprised when Allie barged in without waiting for an invitation.

"We have a question for you," Allie said.

Anna couldn't tell if Allie looked more hurt or angry.

"Anna can explain it better than I can," Allie said, as soon as the three of them sat in the living room.

Violet still hadn't said a word.

"As you know, we've been doing a little investigating into Chester's murder," Anna said, calmly.

"Are you still doing that?" Violet asked indignantly. "I really wish you would leave the investigating to the police. It sounds like dangerous business to me."

Anna ignored Violet's comment. "There are a few questions that came up during some of our recent conversations, and we were hoping you could provide some answers."

HOT FUDGE HOMICIDE

"I'll do my best, but I really do think you should stay out of this. We have a wonderful police department, and we pay good taxes to have them."

"Aunt Violet, please just answer Anna's questions. For Jackson and me."

Violet let out an exasperated sigh. "Go ahead."

"We've learned a few things over the past five days," Anna continued. "First, many people who spent time with Chester noticed that he was getting more short-tempered and agitated in the last couple of months. People noticed that you seemed to be taking the brunt of his unpleasant behavior, but that it didn't seem to rattle you. You were more attentive toward him than ever before."

Violet looked at Allie, then back to Anna and Todd. "I think people's imaginations are running wild. Chester was not the easiest person to live with, but he was simply behaving the way he always had. I would know."

"That's not all," Anna said. "Todd and I spoke with both Dorothea and Eliza. Dorothea said that she confided in you that she lost a large sum of money when she invested in one of Chester's unsuccessful real estate investments. Dorothea said that when she told you what happened, you told her not to worry about it. You promised her that the situation would resolve itself soon. And then when Eliza told you she wanted to quit working for Chester and that Chester wouldn't let her, you asked her to hang in there a little longer, and you again promised that the situation would resolve itself."

"I simply believed that it would all work out in the end," Violet said. She shifted in her chair.

"I'm sorry, Violet, but that seems like too much of a coinci-

95

dence. It was as if you knew what was going to happen to Chester," Anna said.

Tears were now streaming down Allie's face. "Aunt Violet, I know he was difficult. I imagine that living with him could feel downright impossible. But please tell me that you didn't kill him. There had to be an easier way to deal with him. Couldn't you have just asked for a divorce?"

"And that's not all," Anna said. "Chester's hot fudge sundae was likely tampered with when he was in the kitchen getting some water. As far as we can figure, he went into the butler's pantry, where Allie and Jackson kept the water cooler, and probably left his sundae on the table. That's when the killer had to have poured the poisoned fudge onto his sundae. One of the guests saw you follow Chester into the kitchen."

At this point, Allie had worked herself into a frenzy. "I already lost my parents, and now Uncle Chester is gone, too. There aren't a lot of people in the family left in your generation. I don't want to lose you to prison."

Violet stood up and sat next to Allie on the couch. The emotion that had filled Violet's eyes revealed that Allie's words touched her deeply. "Of course not, child. I'm not going to prison. Will you look at me?"

Violet took a tissue from a box on the coffee table and handed it to Allie, who hesitantly looked up. "You know that despite everything, I loved Chester and I love this family." Violet let out a long sigh. "There's something that Uncle Chester and I were keeping secret. After he died, I wasn't sure whether to reveal it to the family, but it seems like I have no choice now."

Allie had calmed down and was listening.

"A little over a month ago, Uncle Chester and I received

some devastating news. He went to the doctor, because he was experiencing headaches and memory issues. They ran a series of tests and scans, and we learned that Chester had a brain tumor. It was late stage, and the doctors told him he didn't have long to live."

"Why didn't you tell us?" Allie asked.

"That was your uncle's wish. He wanted things to remain normal for as long as possible. I encouraged him to tell a few people, at least, but he was a stubborn man and there was nothing I could say to change his mind. I had no choice but to respect his wishes. That's why he was so short-tempered lately, and that's also why I was able to find the patience to deal with it. I knew where it was coming from. He was struggling with having received a terminal diagnosis, and he was frustrated with the memory and judgment issues he was experiencing."

"So, that's why you told Eliza and Dorothea that their situations would resolve themselves," Anna said.

"Yes. I knew that I would eventually pay back the investors who lost money in that investment and that Eliza would be able to accept a new job. I believed that if they knew the situation, they would have been more patient with Chester. I just couldn't tell them. I came close a few times, but in the end, I decided to respect my husband's wishes. With Chester's memory problems, I knew that it wouldn't be long until I took over the finances and that I would simply reimburse Dorothea, Nick, and the others the money they had lost in that bad business deal. That's why I asked them to trust me and assured them that everything would resolve itself in due time. I had a conversation with Eliza just before Chester received his diagnosis, and she told me that she was concerned about a few decisions he had made recently. That was one of the reasons I took him to the doctor for tests. Chester's mind had always been so sharp, especially when it came to business. The doctors told us that the tumor could affect his judgment, but Chester didn't believe them. He was still in denial. But I knew what was happening."

Anna glanced at Allie, who appeared stunned, then at Todd, who appeared equally surprised.

That was not the answer that any of them expected.

Violet continued, "In hindsight, I can see how that must have looked to Eliza and Dorothea after Chester was murdered. I can only imagine what they must think of me. Before now, I hadn't given it much thought. I think I'll pay them both a visit and explain everything. The wake is tomorrow, and I want all this to be cleared up before then."

A relieved Allie hugged her aunt. "I'm so sorry that I thought the worst. Can you ever forgive me?"

"Of course," Violet said with a reassuring smile. "Under the circumstances, we're all a bit on edge. And I certainly didn't help the matter by not telling you about Chester's illness."

"Poor Uncle Chester," Allie said. "I know that he didn't have much time left, but whoever killed him robbed him of the little time he did have with his family. I can't decide if this makes me feel better about what happened, or worse. Anna, I hope you can get to the bottom of this for us."

That also explained why Violet had been watching Chester like a hawk at the party. She wasn't looking for an opportunity to poison him. She was keeping an eye on him, because she knew he was sick.

"Thank you for telling us the truth," Anna said. "I just have one more question. Was there anyone else in the kitchen while Chester was getting his water?"

"I did hear someone come into the kitchen, but I don't know who it was. I accompanied Chester into the butler's pantry while he got his water. I heard someone in the kitchen, but the person was gone by the time we returned to the main part of the kitchen. I should have told you that I went into the kitchen with Chester, instead of lying and saying that I went to the restroom. But I didn't want you or the police wasting time investigating me."

CHAPTER 14

After they left Violet's house, Todd drove Allie and Anna back to Anna's house, where Allie had left her car. None of them spoke until Todd had parked on the street in front of Anna's cottage.

Allie finally broke the silence. "I have to say, I'm relieved that the killer isn't Aunt Violet. I mean, I could never imagine someone as sweet as her doing such a thing, but when you guys told me what Eliza and Dorothea both said, it made her look so guilty."

"It certainly did," Todd said. "Violet was going around telling people that their problems with Chester would soon be over, then the man ends up poisoned to death. I truly thought we had solved the case. I couldn't imagine that there could be another explanation for her behavior. I guess it's back to the drawing board."

"We know that Aunt Violet didn't do it," Allie said. "But we still don't know who did."

"We didn't tell you this earlier because we were so focused on Violet," Anna said. "But when Todd and I spoke with Eliza, we learned something interesting about Drake. Eliza caught him searching your uncle's files one morning when she arrived at the office. Drake was looking for information on the recent real estate investment that tanked. According to Eliza, he was snapping photos of the documents in the file."

"Why do you suppose he was doing that?" Allie asked.

"I don't know for sure, but when Eliza was putting away the file, she said that she looked at the names of the investors, and Nick was listed. Maybe Drake was trying to get more information for his father," Anna said.

"Why wouldn't Uncle Nick have told us that he was one of the investors?" Allie asked.

"We're wondering the same thing," Anna said.

"It sounds like we need to talk to both Drake and Nick again," Todd said.

"The wake and funeral are tomorrow and Saturday, so they'll obviously be tied up during those days," Allie said.

"Why don't we connect after that and come up with our next move?" Anna suggested to Todd.

"That works for me," Todd said.

They all went their separate ways. Since Anna couldn't do anything about Chester's investigation for the next couple of days, and it was still early, she decided to take drive up to Maine to hit a few more salons. She pulled out her list and decided on four salons located in Portland, just a little further north than Kennebunk.

The drive north reminded Anna that she hadn't visited her parents in a while. She made a mental note to call them and arrange a visit. The fall was one of her favorite times to visit them in New Hampshire.

It was early afternoon when Anna arrived in Portland. She

had put the address to *Nailed It!*, the first salon she planned to visit today, into her GPS, and it brought her to a parking lot outside a salon just a few minutes off the highway.

Anna suddenly got butterflies. She missed Jeremy's support. Taking a deep breath, Anna got out of the car, and she rehearsed her story in her mind: She was a high school classmate of Izzy. Anna is president of the class, and they are throwing a class reunion in the spring. Anna doesn't know Izzy's last name, because she heard she was married after high school, but Izzy didn't keep in touch with anyone. Another classmate said she worked as a nail technician at a salon in Portland. Would this by chance be the salon where Izzy worked?

Easy peasy.

Anna took another deep breath and entered the salon.

The receptionist looked at Anna's nails. "Manicure?"

Anna looked down at her nails. She had chipped one the previous day, so she could use a manicure. But now was not the time. "Maybe another time. I'm actually looking for a friend who may work here." Anna gave the receptionist her spiel and asked if a nail technician named Izzy worked there.

The receptionist shook her head then turned around and addressed the two technicians who were giving pedicures to two chatty women. "Tanya, Deb, do either of you know a nail technician in town named Izzy? This woman is looking for her for a class reunion."

They both said that they didn't.

"Sorry. There are a few other salons in town," the receptionist said. "You could try those."

"Thanks," Anna said, and left.

She crossed *Nailed It!* off her list and drove to the next

establishment on her list, *Lucy's Spa*. There was no receptionist at the desk, but a few technicians were working on
clients. Anna said the same thing she had said at the previous
salon and got a similar reaction.

"Sorry. Don't know any nail technician named Izzy," one
of the women said.

The others shook their heads.

Anna thanked them and left, feeling as if she wasn't going
to find Bella in Portland. She tried to imagine Jeremy sitting
next to her and cheering her on. She set her nose to the grind-
stone and pushed on to the last two salons.

However, as Anna suspected, Bella wasn't at either of
them, and nobody had heard of her. None of the people she
talked to appeared the least bit nervous or anxious when
Anna asked about Izzy, so she had no reason to believe they
weren't telling the truth. At least she could check four more
salons off her list. And it was good to know that her cover
story wasn't raising any eyebrows.

There were still twelve salons on her list. Even though it
felt like a wasted day, Anna took comfort in telling herself
that she *had* to be narrowing in on her sister.

While she was driving home, Anna called her mom. She
couldn't help but notice that ever since March, when Anna
moved to Seagull Cove, her parents had hardly visited. They
came to see her cottage when she first bought it, and again for
the grand opening of *Bella's Dream*, but other than those two
times, they seemed to always have an excuse not to come.
Anna guessed that the reason was because Bella's boating
accident took place in Seagull Cove, but Anna was still disappointed.

Besides, Anna was just as guilty, especially now that she

was searching for Bella. She knew she was visiting her parents less frequently, because she hated having to lie about Bella, even if it was a lie of omission. When Bella's name would inevitably come up in conversation, Anna couldn't help but want to blurt out that Bella might not have died in that accident, after all. Especially to her older brother, Albie. Anna was paranoid that Albie would know something was up. She never could pull anything past him. Then again, they had no way of knowing what was going on.

She knew Bella was alive somewhere. At least, she was reasonably certain. What on earth could have happened that left Bella with no option but to fake her own death?

Anna's mother, Judy, answered cheerily. "Hi, Anna."

The fact that her mother seemed so happy to hear Anna's voice made her feel guilty for not calling and visiting more often.

"What are you up to today? Are you at work?" Judy asked.

Oh, great. A few seconds into the conversation, and she already had to lie.

"No, I'm in my car right now. I was just running some errands and realized that I haven't called in a while."

"It's good to hear your voice, sweetheart," she said. "You know, Albie, Christine, and Sophia are coming to Sunday dinner this weekend. Would you by chance be able to come?" Christine was Albie's wife, and Sophia was their sixteen-year-old daughter.

Anna's parents had retired to Windham, New Hampshire a few years ago, which was about an hour-and-a-half from Seagull Cove. Anna had no excuse for not visiting.

She couldn't avoid Sunday dinners forever. She would just have to figure out a better way to handle things.

"Sure, Mom, I think I can manage that. The usual time?"

"Yes. 2:00."

"Your father and Albie will be thrilled. I can't wait to tell them. I'll let you get back to your errands. We'll catch up on Sunday," Judy said before disconnecting the call.

Anna had to smile at her mother's exuberance. It felt nice to be missed. She glanced at the clock on her dashboard. With traffic, she would be driving for at least another hour-and-a-half. She should have downloaded some podcasts to listen to on the drive.

There was one person she had been meaning to call, but she kept putting it off, because she knew it would be a long conversation. Since she had the time, she decided to give it a try.

Anna was thrilled when her cousin picked up after the first ring.

"Anna McBride!"

"Connie! I've been meaning to call for so long."

CHAPTER 15

"It's great to hear from you," Connie said. "I was afraid you might be working."

"Nope. Your timing is perfect. I'm just sitting on the beach in front of my condo. I decided to take the afternoon off while I still can. It's still pretty quiet here in southwest Florida. Some of the snowbirds are beginning to return, but we're still quite a few months out from the high season."

"Ah, yes. I always forget that our busy seasons are at opposite times of the year," Anna said. "Summers are busy here in New England, and winters are slow. But in Sapphire Beach, all the tourists and snowbirds head south in the winter and leave for the oppressive summer months."

"What are you up to this afternoon?" Connie asked.

Anna chuckled. "I'm driving back to Seagull Cove from Portland, Maine. It's kind of a long story."

"I've been meaning to call you to get an update of what we talked about in June. Does your excursion to Maine have anything to do with Bella, by any chance?"

"It does. I'm sorry I haven't updated you. It's been crazy-busy here. But a lot has happened on that front since we last spoke."

"You're kidding," Connie said. "I figured you hadn't made much progress, since I haven't heard from you."

"It's just been so hectic between it being high season here and everything else going on."

Connie chuckled. "Yes, I heard you've gotten involved in a few more murder investigations."

"I have. I think of you all the time as I get sucked into them."

"That's what happens. They draw you in."

"Or the loved ones of the victim draws you in," Anna added.

"It's always something. Anyway, tell me about Bella. The last we talked, your friend, Joe Wiggins, thought he saw Bella across the street the morning of your grand opening. Then the two of you took a boat out to the site of Bella's accident. Joe told you that if Bella had wanted to stage her death, that would be a good place to do it, because it was near a residential area where she could have easily escaped undetected."

"Yes. Those two things are what got me to go full force into investigating. But there have been several more developments since then. Connie, it looks like Bella is alive."

There was silence on the other end of the phone.

"Connie, are you there?"

"Anna, what makes you say that?" Connie asked in a choked-up voice.

"Let me start from the beginning." Over the next half hour, Anna filled Connie in on finding the financial records that indicated a large unaccounted-for withdrawal from Bella's savings and retirement accounts shortly before her accident;

how Bella's boyfriend, Greyson, told Anna that Bella was taking nail technician classes before her accident but that Bella kept this a secret from Anna; how Anna and Jeremy had visited *Castleton Beauty School* and the reaction they got from Justine when they showed her a picture of Bella; how Justine called Bella 'Izzy,' but then suddenly pretended she didn't know who Bella was, and the similar reaction Anna and Jeremy received from Carly when Anna mentioned *Castleton*.

"The look of recognition on Justine's face when I showed her the photo of Bella was unmistakable. She identified her as Izzy without hesitation. Then, a few seconds later, she completely changed her story. Carly pretty much did the same thing. Connie, it all adds up. I know she is alive somewhere, likely somewhere in Maine. Why else would Bella have crossed the state border to get her license to be a nail technician? Joe Wiggins obtained a list of salons and spas where *Castleton* grads have obtained employment upon graduation. Today, I visited another four schools in Portland."

"You think Bella took these classes to have a skill to fall back on, because she knew she would fake her death?"

"I mean, it makes sense. She couldn't practice psychology, because her license is under her real name."

"True. How did you originally figure out she was in Maine?" Connie asked.

"I found a credit card receipt for a restaurant in southern Maine on a Thursday evening the spring before Bella disappeared. That's the night Greyson said that Bella was taking classes. *Castleton* was the nearest school, which is why Jeremy and I started there. Now, I'm visiting the salons on the list Joe compiled, hoping that she works in one of those salons, or at least someone who works at one of them knows where I can find her. It's tricky, though, because anyone who knew her from *Castleton* clams right up when we mention her name. Jeremy and I are convinced that she made up some story about why she doesn't want to be found. So, I stopped mentioning *Castleton*. That's when I made up the story about going to high school with Bella and wanting to find her to invite her to an upcoming reunion."

There was a brief silence. It was a lot to process, so Anna gave Connie a minute.

"I can't believe this, Anna. We might actually see Bella again!"

"I know it's a lot to process. But you have to promise me that you won't tell anyone. The only other people I've confided in are Joe and Jeremy, because I need their help. If Bella staged her death, she had to have had a good reason. It was obviously a matter of life and death. I don't mind telling you, because you live far away, so I doubt it would put you in danger. Plus, I needed to tell someone in the family. I was considering telling Gianna, but I don't want to take that risk. At least not until I know more about the situation."

Gianna was Connie's younger sister.

"Promise me that you'll be really careful, Anna. You don't know who or what you're dealing with. I'm usually on the receiving end of that advice, but it can't be emphasized enough."

"I know. Joe and Jeremy are both making sure of that. Not to mention Charlie, the local detective. He laid the guilt on thick, making me think about how awful it would be for my family to tragically lose someone else."

"He's right. I want to meet these guys. Especially Jeremy.

There's something about the sound of your voice when you say his name. Is he cute?"

"I can't deny that. But it's not like that between us."

"Maybe it *should* be," Connie teased.

"I'll introduce you to them all the next time you come back to Massachusetts. Any thoughts on when that might be?" Anna asked.

"I'm thinking about coming for Christmas."

Anna couldn't believe her ears. "*This* Christmas?! That's only a couple of months away! That would be amazing!" Anna said. "It will be my first winter in town, but I hear there is a lot to do in Seagull Cove around Christmas. It would be fun to explore it together. That is, if life calms down. In addition to Bella, I have another investigation going on. Now that the slower season is here, I was looking for some ways to drum up some business, so I started offering hot fudge sundae bars. My first clients were a young couple celebrating their first anniversary. At the party, someone poisoned their Uncle Chester's sundae, and he died."

"How awful," Connie said sympathetically.

Anna explained the case.

"It sounds like you're on the right track, focusing on Drake and Nick next," Connie said. "Especially Drake. People don't usually go sneaking around their uncle's office unless they are up to no good."

"That's what Todd said, too."

"Who's Todd?"

"A regular customer who happened to be in the ice cream shop when my employee called in sick. He helped me cover the sundae bar."

"You've been holding out on me, cousin," Connie said.

"You have a lot more going on in your life than you let on. Is this a love triangle?"

"Oh, it's not like that. Honestly, Connie, between my search for Bella - which is the most important thing right now - my business, and the murders that keep happening, the last thing I have the time or emotional energy for is a relationship."

"I get it," Connie said. "That's exactly how I felt when I met Zach. If it's right with either of them, you'll know."

"I'm sure you're right." Anna glanced at the clock on her dashboard. "I can't believe we've been talking for over an hour. I didn't mean to keep you this long."

"Are you kidding? It's great talking with you. We should do it more often. Keep me posted on everything."

"Hopefully, we can catch up in person at Christmastime. Please do your best to come."

"I promise," Connie said. "I'll talk to you soon."

Anna hadn't realized how much she needed to confide in a family member, someone who knew both her and Bella. As a counselor, it was part of the job to keep things confidential, so there were lots of things she didn't talk to her family about. But this was different, because it involved her own life. Anna wanted to scream from the rooftops that her sister might be alive. But she couldn't. And talking to Connie helped ease that burden.

By the time she hung up with Connie, Anna was almost back in Seagull Cove. She decided to make one last phone call to Jeremy, to let him know that she had visited four more salons. "I didn't have any success, but the cover story worked well. Nobody questioned it. And at least I crossed a few more salons off the list."

"It sounds like a productive day. Are we still on for Monday?"

"Absolutely. I'll choose a few more salons for us to visit, and we can get back to it then."

"Perfect. I'll pick you up at your house on Monday morning at the usual time."

"See you then."

CHAPTER 16

*A*fter talking with her mom, Connie, and Jeremy, Anna was all talked out.

Her first stop was *Bella's Dream* to check in on her employees. It was a slow evening, and since she was worn out from her phone conversations and the drive, Anna headed home for the night. She took a walk to stretch her legs after the long drive and spent the evening relaxing on her couch.

Since there wasn't much she could do about the case for the next couple of days because of Chester's wake and funeral, Anna spent Friday and Saturday getting ahead on paperwork at *Bella's Dream.*

On Saturday evening, Anna took a half gallon of maple walnut ice cream for her parents, since she would be visiting them the following day. She thought they might enjoy a taste of fall. Although, if she knew her mom, her parents' kitchen would already be stocked with fall goodies.

Anna went to an early Mass on Sunday, then headed north to Windham, New Hampshire.

Her parents, Albert and Judy, owned a detached townhome, which backed onto a densely wooded conservation area. The sweet smells of apple and cinnamon had greeted Anna as she walked through the front door.

Sunlight poured in through the large windows overlooking the woods, and the oak floors reflected the colors of the foliage.

Anna took a moment to take in the array of colors. "I forgot how beautiful this place is in the fall." She handed her mother the ice cream she had brought. "It's beautiful in Seagull Cove, too, but you have so many more trees up north."

"It's one of the reasons we moved here," Albert said.

Anna's mother picked up a ladle and filled a mug with hot apple cider, which had been warming on the stovetop. Then she popped a cinnamon stick into the mug.

Next to the pot of cider was another large stainless steel pot filled with her mother's homemade beef stew. "There's also fresh bread baking in the oven," Judy said. "Albie, Christine, and Sophia will be here any minute." Judy put her arm around her daughter and led her to the plush olive green couch in the living room, just a few steps from the dining room.

From the cushy couch, Anna looked up at the cathedral ceiling boasting dark wooden beams. There was a large window overlooking a group of trees that were ablaze with red, orange, and yellow leaves. As much as Anna loved being by the sea, this area had its own charm.

Anna wondered if Bella lived in a similar kind of home in Maine. Her parents retired to New Hampshire after Bella's accident, so Bella never saw this lovely home. She would love it. For a brief moment, Anna let herself imagine Bella sitting next to her and the two of them talking with their parents.

Judy went into the kitchen to stir the beef stew, and Al stoked the fire that was blazing in the brick fireplace. Then he sat on the couch across from Anna, and Judy joined him.

"Earth to Anna," Al said.

"Sorry, Dad. I guess I let my thoughts wander."

Anna noticed the familiar expression of pain in Judy's eyes. Anna had a feeling that her mother was thinking of Bella, too.

"You know, it's been five years this month since your sister's accident," her mom said.

"I know," Anna said. "I think about her every day. In some ways, it seems like yesterday. But then at other times, it feels like a lifetime ago." That feeling of guilt at not sharing with her parents that she was investigating Bella's accident tugged at her heart, but she quickly pushed it down into the pit of her stomach. She couldn't tell them. For so many reasons.

"Bella would be proud of the business you are building," Al said.

"Thanks, Dad. I think so, too."

"I just wish…" Judy's voice trailed off.

"I know, Mom. I wish she were here, running it with me, too."

Fortunately, Albie and his family arrived, and Judy's spirits lifted.

After greeting Albie, Christine, and Sophia, Judy turned to go into the kitchen.

"Sit down, Mom," Anna said. "You've been cooking all day."

"We've got this," Christine said.

Anna and Christine added beef stew to six bright ceramic bowls painted with flowers, which Judy had set out on the counter, and sliced the bread, still hot from the oven. They placed the stew, bread, and butter dish on the table, which was already set, and sat to enjoy a family meal.

Al invited Sophia to say grace, then they dug into their hearty meals.

The familiar chatter caused Anna to relax. She got caught up on Sophia's soccer season, Albie's work as a veterinarian, and Judy's and Al's new friends, who had moved into the unit next door.

Anna silently chided herself for not coming to visit more frequently. Her brother must have been reading her mind. "Hopefully, now that the holidays are right around the corner, we'll see more of you."

"I wish we lived closer to *Bella's Dream*," Sophia said. "That way I could work in your ice cream shop."

"Sophia just got a job bagging groceries at Market Basket," Albie said proudly.

"That's wonderful," Al said. "I always encouraged you, Anna, and Bella to work as teenagers. It builds character."

Albie and Anna looked at each other and chuckled.

"Actually, Dad, I think you did more than encourage it." Anna recalled her father insisting that she work as soon as she turned sixteen. He stopped paying her an allowance for chores and reminded her that she would have many expenses coming up now that her senior year was approaching.

"I guess you're right. But that's only because it's so important. And look at you now. You're both hard workers who never expected anything to be handed to you."

"I agree," Christine said. "Both Albie and Anna have very strong work ethics, so it obviously worked."

Judy smiled. "Bella did, too."

"Sophia, when you get your license, you can visit once in a while, and I'll give you all the free ice cream you can eat."

"It's a deal. But I'm warning you, after a soccer game, I can eat a lot more than you think."

"I'll take my chances. I doubt you can eat me out of business."

"Don't be so sure," Albie said.

"Speaking of ice cream, I brought some maple walnut. I started carrying it this month, and it seems to be a hit."

After dinner, the family retired to the living room, each with a bowl full of ice cream, and Al added another log to the fireplace.

"So, what is this we hear from Greg and Jo that Anna is Seagull Cove's unofficial amateur sleuth?" Al asked.

Greg was Judy's brother. He was also Connie's and Gianna's father.

"Now we have two in the family," Albie said. "Connie and Anna."

"I don't like it one bit," Judy said. "And neither does Greg. Can't you two find a safer hobby?"

"Don't give her a hard time," Albie said. "We don't see her nearly enough as it is, and the holidays are coming up. We want her around as much as possible."

"Can't a mother express her opinion?"

Anna saw the fear in her mother's eyes. She knew her mother could never handle losing another daughter. But still, Anna needed to follow her own heart.

"It's okay. I don't scare off that easily," Anna said.

"That's not the only thing Greg and Jo told us. Apparently, Connie is considering coming home for Christmas. It's Zach's year to work, so he can't get the time off this year, but he told

Connie that she should come, anyway. They're going to choose another day to celebrate Christmas."

"I talked to Connie the other day, and she told me she might come. She didn't mention that Zach had to work, though." *Probably because they were too busy talking about investigations,* she thought. "I hope she does. I would love to see her again. Her wedding was almost a year ago. It would be great to catch up."

"We all do," Judy said. "I will keep it in my prayers. For all the good *that* will do."

Anna looked at her mother, shocked. "What do you mean?"

"Oh, I'm sorry. I didn't mean to be negative like that. Of course I believe that my prayers are heard. It's just with Bella's fifth anniversary being this month, I guess I'm feeling a little sorry for myself. God knows that I prayed so hard in the days after her accident that the coast guard would find her alive."

Anna's heart ached to tell her mother what she knew. She had to bite her tongue so hard to refrain from blurting it all out that she almost drew blood.

Albie put his arm around his mother's shoulders and gave them a squeeze.

By the time Anna left, she was more determined than ever to find her sister. Not that she needed any additional motivation.

CHAPTER 17

*A*nna drove home from Sunday dinner with her family feeling more at peace than she had felt in a long time. She was beginning to get excited for the upcoming holidays.

It was early in the evening, but Anna decided to go straight home rather than stop at work.

It had been a crisp, sunny day, but the temperature was dropping as the sun went down. Anna glanced at the wood-burning fireplace in her living room. Inspired by the roaring fire at her parents' home, she decided that tonight was the perfect night to use hers. A fireplace had been a non-negotiable on her wish list when searching for the perfect home in Seagull Cove. The image she had of herself, sitting in front of a blazing fire with a large steaming mug, was not one she had been willing to compromise. Now seemed like the perfect evening to bring that image from fantasy to reality.

She added a log to the fireplace grate and surrounded it with pinecones she had collected and placed in a basket next to the fireplace for just such a time. Then she lit it and waited for the log to catch fire.

As it grew to a roar, her cell phone rang. It was Todd.

"Hi, Anna. I just stopped by your ice cream shop, but you weren't there. I was hoping you might have some time to talk about our next move with the investigation."

"Hi, Todd. I just returned from visiting my parents in New Hampshire. I'm just relaxing by the fire."

"Would you mind if I came over so we could talk about the case?" he asked.

Anna had been looking forward to a quiet evening at home, but they really did need to get their heads back in the game. They hadn't done anything since their conversation with Violet.

"Sure," Anna said. "We should get back to it. Besides, it's the first time I've used this fireplace since I moved here, so if my house should catch fire, it will be good to have someone to help me put it out."

"Happy to help... I think," Todd said.

Within ten minutes, Todd Devonshire was sitting on one of Anna's oversized armchairs with a cup of hot cider. Her mother had sent her home with a gallon of cider from a local orchard, so Anna had heated some up for herself and Todd.

"This is nice," he said. "You have a beautiful home."

Anna remembered that Velma had told her that, judging from Todd's address, he lived in a mansion in Gloucester. She couldn't tell if Todd was being polite or sincere, but she gave him the benefit of the doubt and accepted the compliment.

"Thank you. I love living in Seagull Cove. I always dreamed of living in a cottage like this one."

Todd lifted his mug in a toast. "Here's to meeting our goals."

"Speaking of goals, we should figure out our next move with Chester's investigation."

"Wow, you're focused. I like that in a person. Okay. Chester."

"Let's go over what we know," Anna said. "First, we know it had to be someone in Allie's family who was at the party. And we know that Violet didn't do it. Her motive would have been to get rid of Chester so she could collect her inheritance and no longer have to put up with his ill-tempered behavior. Chester was terminally ill, so Violet would have inherited his money shortly, anyway, and she wouldn't have to live with him much longer."

"That leaves Drake, Nick, Eliza, and Dorothea," Todd said.

"It could be any of them, really. Drake and Nick seem like they have the most tumultuous history with Chester. Chester manipulated Drake by forcing him to choose a path in life that he didn't want. And Drake had to hide his writing career from Chester in order to remain in the will. Maybe he got tired of living a lie," Anna said. "Since his first book seems to have been a success, and he just released his second, maybe he realized that he had a chance at becoming a successful author. His inheritance money from Chester would certainly help with that."

"Or he could have simply been tired of being pushed around by his uncle," Todd added. "Then there's Nick. He, too, seemed fed up with Chester."

"True. Maybe watching Chester control his son's life and taking Chester's insults got to be too much. Maybe Nick wanted an escape for both of them but didn't want to give up

121

his inheritance. And since Nick lost money in Chester's recent investment, he could have decided to take matters into his own hands and get his inheritance from Chester early," Anna said.

"That's definitely possible. Anna, there's something else I want to tell you. I was debating whether I should bring it up, and I'm not sure if I should do anything about it, but I wanted to tell you, anyway."

"What is it?" Anna asked.

"I knew that Chester's last name, Corbyn, sounded familiar. I racked my brain trying to figure out why all week. Last night, I was skimming through some old work files, and I finally figured it out. Oliver Corbyn, Drake's brother, is a former client. It could be helpful for us to talk to him, but I'm not sure if it would be right for me to call him."

"I understand your dilemma. Oliver might know something that could help us, but I wouldn't want you to breach your professional ethics."

"It's a tough call. Oliver isn't a current client, so technically, there's no conflict of interest. And I could explain that he's under no obligation to talk with us," Todd said.

"It sounds like you're leaning towards giving Oliver a call," Anna said.

"I think I am."

"For what it's worth, I don't see a problem with it. He's no longer a client, and you're not using any information that you learned about him through your business interactions with him. As you said, he can always say no."

"True. Okay. I'll give him a call tomorrow and see if I can set up a time for us to talk with him. It's going to be touchy, though. What are we supposed to say? Could you tell us anything that might help prove that your brother or father killed your uncle?"

Anna chuckled. "We'll definitely need another approach. We can start by focusing on Eliza and Dorothea. We'll have to be discreet in the way we bring up the others, though."

"I guess it's worth a shot," Todd said. "From what I remember, Oliver's a pretty reasonable guy." Todd glanced at his Piaget watch. "I should get going. I don't want to take up any more of your quiet evening."

"Thanks for coming, Todd. I'll sleep better knowing we have a plan."

As Todd stood to leave, the doorbell rang.

"I wonder who that could be," Anna said, walking to the door.

She opened it to find Jeremy Russo carrying a white pastry box.

"Hi, Anna. I'm sorry to drop by without calling, but I'm afraid I have to work tomorrow so I can't help with Bella's…"

Anna held up her hand to silence Jeremy just as Todd walked up behind her.

CHAPTER 18

"Oh, excuse me. I didn't realize you had company," Jeremy said.

Todd and Jeremy exchanged a glance that Anna couldn't quite make out. If she didn't know any better, they were sizing each other up.

"It's okay. I was just leaving. It was nice seeing you again, Anna," Todd said. "I'll call you tomorrow."

Todd left with a smirk, and Jeremy looked at Anna and then back at the roaring fireplace and the two mugs of cider. She couldn't help but notice the hurt expression that crept onto his face.

"I thought you told me you weren't looking to date anyone right now."

"It's not what it looks like," Anna said. She somewhat resented explaining herself to Jeremy, since they weren't in a relationship. But he *was* becoming a good friend. "Todd and I were talking about Chester and trying to come up with our next move. It's still true that I have too much on my plate right now for a relationship with anyone."

"Anna, *you* may only be focused on the investigation into Chester's death, but don't be so sure that he doesn't have anything else in mind."

Anna waved away his comment. And she tried to forget that Velma had just implied the same thing about Todd.

"Sorry about the Bella comment," Jeremy said. "I shouldn't have assumed that you were alone. His car looked like it was parked in front of Wanda's house, not yours."

"That's okay. I don't think Todd picked up on it. Were you starting to say that you couldn't come to Maine tomorrow?" Anna asked.

"Oh, right. That's why I came. I brought these apple turnovers as an apology. The police are giving a statement about Chester's murder tomorrow, and I need to stay in town so I can be present. It's scheduled for 1:00, which would cut too much into our time. Besides, these things never happen on schedule. I should be able to take Thursday off instead, though. Are you free then?"

"That will work," Anna said. "I'll go alone tomorrow. I want to get through these salons as quickly as possible. Then I'll go again with you on Thursday. Unless I should find Bella tomorrow, that is."

"Okay. Again, I'm sorry to cancel at the last minute. Let me know if you learn anything interesting," Jeremy said.

"I will." Anna smiled playfully. "Speaking of Chester's investigation, have you learned anything you care to share?"

"I'll share what I know, if you do," Jeremy said.

"As long as it's off the record." At this point, she trusted Jeremy enough to know that his word was as good as gold.

"Of course."

Anna looked at the box of apple turnovers. Their sweet

scent had already made its way to her nostrils. "I'm not going to be able to resist these. Would you like to have one with me now?"

Jeremy smiled. "You don't have to ask me twice."

Between all the cider and dessert that she had eaten today, Anna doubted her sugar rush would ever wear off. What was one more dessert? She placed two of the four apple turnovers that Jeremy had brought into plates.

"Would you like some tea?" Anna asked from the kitchen.

"How about a glass of milk?"

Anna poured two glasses of cold milk, put the glasses and plates on a tray, and brought them into the living room.

"Do you think the police are close to an arrest?" Anna asked.

"I'm not sure. However, a source told me that Chester may have had a terminal illness. If that was common knowledge among his family and friends, then most of them no longer have a motive to kill him. The police would be back at square one."

"I can save you some guesswork on that," Anna said. "Chester had terminal brain cancer, but Violet is the only one who knew. Chester had asked her not to tell anyone."

"You're sure about that?"

"Positive. Violet told me herself. Allie, Todd, and I pressed her, because she was looking more and more guilty. She came clean on Chester's illness. Since he was dying, Violet no longer has a motive, but none of the others knew about his illness, so their motives still hold."

Anna updated Jeremy on what she had learned about Nick, the investment gone bad, and Eliza wanting to quit.

"Did you say that Dorothea had invested in Chester's building project?" Jeremy asked.

"Both Dorothea and Nick," Anna said. "Dorothea apparently invested a good chunk of her retirement in the project."

"That's interesting. I know Dorothea from church. I saw her working in a retail store just outside of town last month. We chatted for a bit, and she told me that her retirement investments weren't doing well, so she needed a part-time job to help make ends meet. I went back yesterday, and one of the other employees told me she no longer works there. I was wondering what happened."

"Hmmm, that is interesting. I know that when Chester's real estate investment went south, Dorothea told Violet about it. Violet assured her that the situation would resolve itself and not to worry. At the time, Dorothea thought that was a strange thing, especially after Chester was murdered. But Violet simply meant that she planned to pay back the investors the money they lost from Chester's business once she inevitably took over their finances. Perhaps Violet reimbursed her already. Nobody could understand why Chester would make such a bad investment, but now they know that the tumor had affected his judgement."

"Poor Violet. You have to admire her for reimbursing the investors. Legally, she doesn't have to do that."

When they finished their turnovers, Anna walked Jeremy to his car. As she was walking back up the stairs of her porch, Wanda's door opened. Daniel was leaving, and Wanda was walking him out.

Daniel waved and Anna waved back.

"Two gentleman callers in one night?" he asked with a smirk.

Wanda whacked him across the shoulder. "That's none of our business, Daniel Appleton."

"Ouch," he said, rubbing his shoulder. "I didn't mean anything by it. I think it's good. Anna's young. She should enjoy life."

Anna smiled. "Thanks for calling me young, but it's not what it looks like."

"Well, it's none of our business either way," Wanda said, looking sideways at Daniel.

He laughed and gave Wanda a kiss on the cheek before he descended Wanda's porch steps and got into his car.

It took Anna a while to fall asleep because of all the sugar she had consumed that day, but it was worth it.

When she awoke on Monday morning, she had a quick breakfast and headed to Maine. Anna texted Velma to let her know she wouldn't be in. It felt good to take two days off in a row. After the long days of summer, it was nice to spend time away from the shop.

This time, Anna headed to Ogunquit, where a few salons on Joe's list were located. When she was halfway there, there was a sign made from a piece of weathered wood on the side of the road that said 'Farmstand.' Anna couldn't resist making a quick stop for some more fresh produce.

She arrived in Ogunquit in the late morning and hit her first salon. Then her second. And finally, the third on her list. She received much the same response as her previous trip, except this time the receptionist at the final salon convinced her to stay for a manicure and pedicure.

"Why not?" Anna asked. "I have some time."

As Anna was choosing a color, she glanced out the window

at a maple tree and chose an orange that matched the color of some of its leaves.

"Good choice," the technician, who introduced herself as Michaela, said. "Fall only comes once a year."

Anna sat in the pedicure chair and tried to let her thoughts wander to Chester's case, but Michaela insisted on making small talk. "How long ago did you hear that your friend from high school was a nail technician in this town?"

She had been lost in thought, and it took Anna a second realize that Michaela was talking about Bella.

"Oh, it was sometime last year," Anna said, making up a timeframe on the spot.

"You know, nail technicians come and go. A lot of people try it for a while and realize it's not for them. Or they do it for a while, then move on to something else. There's a high turnover rate in this industry, so don't be disappointed if you're not able to find your friend."

Anna's heart sank. Michaela was right. All Anna was reasonably certain of was that Bella attended *Castleton Beauty School*. She may have tried the business out for a while and then moved on to something else.

"I suppose you could be right," Anna said, while at the same time saying a silent prayer that Michaela was wrong.

While Michaela finished Anna's nails, Anna did her best to push out of her mind what Michaela had said. *Castleton* was Anna's only real lead, so she had no choice but to follow where the path took her. However, she was already more than halfway through the salons on the list Joe had furnished her with. What if she got to the end only to find herself back at square one?

She was glad that Jeremy would be coming with her on her next trip. She could use the moral support.

While Anna drove back to Seagull Cove, Todd called. "Good news. We have an appointment with Oliver tomorrow at 10:00. We're meeting him at his office."

"Great. I'll see you then."

At least she received one promising piece of news that day.

CHAPTER 19

Anna stopped at *Bella's Dream* when she returned home from Maine. Velma's and Kathy's shift was ending, and Mary and Sarah were arriving for the closing shift.

"I'm glad to see you're taking some time off," Velma said. "You put in so many hours over the summer that I was afraid you'd burn out."

"I guess I'm finally finding the right work-life balance," Anna said.

Anna stayed until the evening shift employees were settled in. Then, she reminded them to feed Casper at the end of the night, and she returned home.

There was still some time before the sun would go down, and Anna felt like doing something active after all the time she spent in her car that day. She grabbed a rake from her garage and got to work on the front lawn. After an hour of raking, she managed to fill a paper bag with dry leaves.

She returned the rake, along with her newly filled bag, to the garage. When she returned, it took her a moment to notice Wanda standing on the other side of the fence. Anna gasped and put her hand on her chest.

"I didn't mean to scare you. I saw you working in the yard, and I wanted to apologize for Daniel's comment last night about your, um, gentlemen friends."

Anna wanted to laugh, because the comment hadn't bothered her at all. She knew Daniel was just joking around with her. But Wanda's expression was so earnest that Anna did her best to take her concern seriously. "Don't even mention it. It didn't bother me in the least."

Wanda didn't turn immediately to leave, so Anna guessed she might want some company. "Speaking of my friends, one of them brought me some apple turnovers, and I still have a couple left. Would you care to join me for one?"

"Don't mind if I do," Wanda said, scurrying over to the front gate leading into Anna's yard. "It might kill my dinner appetite, but we have to enjoy the fruits of the season while we can."

"My thoughts exactly." Anna brewed some herbal tea and spread a yellow Provençal tablecloth with a red and purple floral print on her table.

Wanda had never invited Anna inside her own home, but Anna was happy that Wanda was at least accepting more invitations into her home than she refused. She enjoyed Wanda's company. Anna had the feeling that Wanda was somewhat of a kindred spirit, although she had to admit, she still knew very little about her neighbor.

"I had a nice visit with my parents yesterday," Anna said. "My brother and his family came, as well."

"They live in New Hampshire, right?"

"Yes. My parents retired to Windham a few years ago. Albie, Christine, and Sophia live in North Andover."

"Do you get up to see your parents often?" Wanda asked.

"Not as much as I should. Growing up, our family vacationed in Seagull Cove. For a few years, my parents even rented a cottage right by Mile Long Beach for all of July and August. My father would commute to his job in Burlington from here. We all loved it. I thought they would visit me more often after I moved here, especially during the summer. But they didn't."

Wanda pressed her lips together before speaking. "Wasn't it just off the shores of Seagull Cove that your sister had her boating accident?"

Anna nodded. "I'm guessing that's why they don't come. I guess it's too hard for them to visit me here. Even Albie doesn't come, although I try to rationalize that by telling myself he is just busy with his veterinarian practice and family life. When I decided to move here, it didn't occur to me that it might be hard on my family. It brings me such solace to be here, where my sister and I shared so many happy memories."

Wanda listened thoughtfully. "I can understand how they might feel that way. Everyone handles grief differently. Take Daniel and me…"

Anna looked at Wanda and tried to hide her surprise at Wanda's candor. She had never shared anything too personal with Anna, but Anna never took it personally. She knew Wanda was like that with everyone.

Wanda paused, and Anna waited in silence to see if she would continue.

Wanda wrapped both hands around her mug, as if holding

on to a dear friend. Then she changed course a bit. "You've probably wondered why Daniel and I don't live together."

Anna gave Wanda a slight nod. "He seems like a good man."

Wanda smiled like a schoolgirl. "He is. He has been very patient with me. Don't think I don't appreciate that." The smile faded from her lips. "You see, Daniel and I had a son named Danny. We had hoped to have more children, but it just wasn't to be for us. We prayed for many years after Danny was born for siblings for our son, but it was a prayer that never was answered. At least not to my satisfaction. I'm not sure I ever forgave God for that."

"I'm sorry," Anna said.

"Thank you. Danny was our whole world. He was good to me and his father, but he had his father's stubborn streak."

Anna suppressed a smile. She had a feeling Danny inherited his stubborn streak equally from both parents.

"Danny was supposed to go to medical school and eventually take over his father's medical practice, but after college, he announced his plan to join the Air Force. He said he intended to go to medical school later, but when he reenlisted after four years, we began to have our doubts." Wanda grew sadder the more she talked. Anna had a feeling she knew where the story was going.

"Shortly after, Danny was sent to Afghanistan for a tour of duty. We were so afraid for his safety, but he assured us that it was where he needed to be. He would write home about his humanitarian efforts and how much he loved helping the local children. He came home and spent some time with us but then announced that he was being sent back for a second tour of duty. That time, he never made it home."

Wanda was gripping her mug so tightly that Anna was afraid she would bruise her hands.

"I'm so sorry, Wanda. Now I understand why you know how hard it is to have a loved one taken much too soon."

Wanda closed her eyes. "I wish I *didn't* know, but I do. I know it's disappointing that your family won't visit you in Seagull Cove, but I can understand where they are coming from. That is why I moved out of Daniel's and my home. That beautiful Victorian home represents the best years of our life. We bought it when Daniel's practice started to take off. Danny was in kindergarten. We had so many happy memories there. Daniel is like you. He prefers to be in that house, with all those memories swirling around, but I just couldn't live among them any longer. I told Daniel that if he wouldn't move out, I was moving out alone. He didn't think I would do it, and after I did, he was too stubborn to admit he should have taken me seriously." Wanda chuckled and shook her head. "I even bought my cottage rather than renting some-where. I bought it with cash that I withdrew from one of our investment portfolios to prove to Daniel how serious I was. Danny was probably laughing at his parents' childish behavior from heaven."

"How long have you lived here?" Anna asked.

"It's been just over two years now. The first year was the hardest, but I threw myself into my gardening and used the alone time to get better. I even started going back to church, once I got over being mad at God and realized I needed him more than I needed to be mad at him. It took a while, though. Eventually, Daniel and I started talking again. He said he'd move in here with me or anywhere else I wanted to live, once he finally understood how hard it was for me to be in that house. But I asked him for more time. I feel like this is where I'm supposed to be right now. I need to be alone for a while. As I said, Daniel is a patient man. He promised he would never give up on us."

Anna had always liked Daniel, but after hearing Wanda's story, she liked him even more.

Wanda had put down the mug and placed her hands on the table. Anna squeezed Wanda's hand. "It seems like we are both here to heal."

Wanda swallowed hard and nodded. "It seems that way."

CHAPTER 20

odd met Anna at her house on Tuesday morning for their meeting with Oliver. Oliver's office was on Main Street, so they opted to walk instead of drive. It took about fifteen minutes, since the office was further north than Anna's shop, but the brisk air felt nice.

Anna and Todd entered the first-floor office suite, where the door was propped open. It was tastefully decorated with a nautical theme that leaned toward the masculine side. A man with sandy blond hair and who appeared to be in his early thirties, dressed in navy pleated pants and a lightweight white sweater came out from one of the offices.

"Hi, Todd," the man said.

Todd stuck out his hand. "Hi, Oliver. It's great to see you again. How's Cheryl?"

"Wonderful. We just got back from a fantastic vacation in Newport."

"Glad to hear it. Your oldest must be in first grade by now," Todd said.

"Yes, yes." Oliver smiled broadly. "She's just started learning to read. It's amazing how quickly it happens."

"I can imagine," Todd said with a charming smile. "I appreciate your taking time out of your busy schedule to meet with us, Oliver." Todd looked Oliver in the eyes. "Especially during such a difficult time."

"Yes," Anna said. "We're sorry for the loss of your uncle."

"Thank you. That's very kind of you both. But I have to admit, I'm a little confused as to why the two of you wanted to talk to me about that."

"I'm not sure how much Todd told you, but we were both at the anniversary party when Chester was killed. I own an ice cream shop and..."

"Oh, which one?" Oliver asked.

"*Bella's Dream.*"

"The one with the open mic nights on Thursday?"

Anna smiled. "Yes."

"My wife and I have been there a couple of times. We love your shop."

"Thank you," Anna said. Oliver didn't look familiar, but some of those open mic nights were busy, and Anna sometimes spent them behind the counter scooping ice cream.

"Allie and Jackson hired Anna to host a hot fudge sundae bar at the party," Todd said.

"What a great idea. It's too bad we had to miss it."

"Well, since it ended in tragedy..." Anna said.

"True. I guess it's good that we weren't there, especially with the kids."

"Anyway," Todd said, "Anna is a friend, and she was short-handed the day of the party, so I went with her to help out.

Anna is pretty upset that the killer used her hot fudge sundae bar to commit such a horrible crime."

"I guess I sort of feel a sense of responsibility to find out who did this," Anna said. "Besides, I have a knack for solving tough crimes."

"Anna has helped the police solve a murder more than once," Todd said.

Three times. Not that Anna was counting.

"That's very impressive. And very kind of you. We appreciate any help you can offer."

"We've talked to Violet, Nick, Drake, Dorothea, and Eliza, along with Allie and Jackson. They seem to be the only ones at the party who knew Chester well enough to have a reason to want him dead."

"Anna, I don't mean to sound callous, but *everybody* Uncle Chester met probably had a motive to want him to go away. I know it sounds harsh, but it's the truth."

"That's what we've been hearing," Todd said.

"The killer had to be at the party, though. I know it's a difficult thing to hear," Anna said, "but it has to be one of the people I mentioned. Allie and Jackson have an alibi, and Violet no longer has a motive."

"On account of Uncle Chester being sick," Oliver said. "Aunt Violet told us all before the wake."

"Right. Violet knew he was dying, so she had no reason to kill him. She would have inherited her share of his fortune before long, anyway."

"That's true. Not that I can imagine Aunt Violet doing something like that, no matter how difficult my uncle was."

"I know it's a difficult thing to think about, but if you had to guess, who do you think had the strongest motive?" Anna asked.

"I'm not as close to the family as I used to be. I never let Uncle Chester manipulate me with his money, and believe me, he tried. I've done pretty well for myself, so I didn't need it. Ironically, he never did cut me out of the will. I think he respected me for putting up boundaries."

"It sounds like Allie is the same way," Anna said.

"She is. And my uncle always had a soft spot for her, probably because he was close with Allie's mother. It made it easier for Allie to stand her ground. But my father and brother gave him too much control. I warned my brother, but he insisted he could have the best of both worlds – that he could remain in Uncle Chester's good graces and still follow his dream."

"Do you think Drake's plan backfired, and he was looking for a way out?" Todd asked.

"I know my uncle was a difficult man, but I never thought anyone would go *that* far."

Oliver seemed to be avoiding the question, not that Anna could blame him. She tried to gently bring him back around to her question. "Allie said the same thing. But someone obviously did. Who do you think is the most likely to have taken matters into their own hands?"

Oliver leaned back in his seat and let out a sigh. "I can't imagine either my father or my brother doing something like that. Neither one of them are confrontational. That's probably why they were more easily manipulated by my uncle. But then again, Drake *has* been acting strangely lately."

"What do you mean by strangely?" Anna probed.

Oliver shrugged his shoulders. "It's hard to explain. He's

seemed cocky lately, especially around Uncle Chester. Like he somehow had the upper hand. You have to understand, we all stood to gain a sizable inheritance. Part of me understands why Drake wanted to have his cake and eat it, too. And with his second book coming out, it looked like he was succeeding. But I have to admit, ever since Uncle Chester's death, I've wondered if that wasn't the only thing he was feeling cocky about."

"Do you mean he might have thought that he literally got away with murder?" Todd asked.

"I can't say the thought hasn't crossed my mind." Then Oliver shook his head. "But no. I know my brother, and I don't think he is capable of murder."

"Did you know that Drake broke into Chester's office, and Eliza caught him reading some files about a real estate investment that went sour?" Anna asked. "Apparently, your father and Dorothea invested in it and lost quite a bit of money. Chester had purchased land using money from investors, and the land turned out to be unbuildable. Everyone was shocked that Chester would invest in a piece of property without doing his due diligence."

Oliver turned white.

"What is it?" Anna asked.

"Are you sure that my father invested it that project?"

"Yes, we're positive."

"So, that's why my father had been so angry with him lately," Oliver said, looking as though he were putting together a puzzle in his mind. "My father didn't tell me the details, but I knew that he recently lost some money in an investment. I should have guessed that the investment was connected to

Uncle Chester. My dad had been avoiding him. He didn't even want to go to the anniversary party, because he knew my uncle would be there, but he didn't have the heart to disappoint Allie and Jackson."

"Dorothea also said that she didn't want to attend the anniversary party, because she was angry with Chester," Todd said. "There had even been talk among the investors that Chester must be up to something shady, since it was so unlike him to make a mistake like that. But now in hindsight, they all understand that the error was due to his medical condition."

"I can see why they would think that. It *was* unlike my uncle to make that kind of a mistake. I guess that makes my father a prime suspect," Oliver said. "If he thought my uncle scammed him out of a chunk of money, that could be interpreted as a motive. But I still say neither of them did it."

Anna didn't doubt Oliver's sincerity, but she knew from past cases that people killed for less.

"I'm sorry I couldn't be more helpful," Oliver said.

"How well do you know Eliza?" Anna asked.

"My uncle's secretary? Fairly well," Oliver said. "She's been a friend of Aunt Violet's for years."

"Apparently she wanted to leave her job, but Chester was making it difficult," Anna said.

"Figures. But she must have succeeded. She got a job offer with another investment firm. I heard she accepted it."

"Yes," Anna said. "Eliza told us that she accepted a new job, now that Chester's office is closing."

Oliver shook his head. "My buddy works at the firm that just hired her, and we had lunch a few weeks ago. Eliza had already accepted that job before my uncle passed. She isn't starting until the first of the year, because their former secretary isn't retiring until then. But as far as accepting the job, that was a done deal weeks ago."

Anna and Todd looked at one another.

"That makes Eliza's motive even stronger," Anna said. "She needed a way out of her current job by the first of the year."

"Perhaps murder was her way out," Todd said.

CHAPTER 21

*A*nna and Todd thanked Oliver for his time and left his office.

"Would you like to get a quick cup of coffee so we can decide what to do next?" Todd asked.

"Sure. I still have a little time before *Bella's Dream* opens."

They ordered their beverages at *Cove Coffee* and grabbed a table by the window.

Sonja was wiping down some empty tables a short distance away. Todd's back was to her, but Anna had a clear view. Sonja took a pen from her pocket and wrote something on a napkin. Then she held it up for Anna to see. "He's cute," it read.

Anna pretended not to see Sonja, who smirked and returned to her cleaning.

"What did you think of our conversation with Oliver?" Todd asked.

"I was surprised that he was willing to speak so openly about his father and Drake. It's one thing to realize that your father or brother could have a motive for murder, but it's quite another to admit that to virtual strangers."

Todd shrugged. "Maybe he figures that if they are innocent, they will be cleared. It's possible that, for his own peace of mind, he wants to know for sure that they didn't do it, and the only way for that to happen is if they are investigated and questioned."

"Hmm, that's an interesting theory."

"I seem to remember Oliver as an ethical guy. When I managed his stock portfolio, there were certain companies he refused to invest in, because their work violated his conscience. It's possible that he trusts the justice system to uncover the truth and appreciates our help in the matter."

"I suppose you could be right."

"Any thoughts on what we should do next?" Todd asked.

"I'll talk to Allie and Jackson to get their thoughts, but I think we should talk to Nick again. We need to find out how much he lost in Chester's scheme. And we need to talk to Drake so we can confront him about why he was snooping in Chester's office."

"Sounds logical. I'll wait for you to be in touch after you talk to Allie and Jackson," Todd said.

After they left the coffee shop, Anna offered to walk Todd back to her house so he could get his car, but Todd insisted that was not necessary. "Your shop is only a couple of doors down from here. There's no need to go out of your way to walk me back."

"All right. I'll talk to you soon, Todd."

Velma was just arriving for work as Anna unlocked the door. "Was that Todd Devonshire?"

"We worked on the case this morning, and we were just discussing it over coffee."

Velma smiled and nodded. "Uh huh."

Kathy came in shortly after Velma, and Anna went back into her office to make some social media posts about upcoming events. About ten minutes later, Anna heard commotion out front, so she went to see what was going on. She found Todd, sweaty and with a panicked expression on his face.

Velma was attempting to calm him down while Kathy was getting him a cup of water.

Fortunately, there were no customers in the shop.

"What's the matter?" Anna asked.

"That's what we're trying to figure out," Velma said.

Todd ran towards Anna when he saw her and put both hands on her shoulders. "Thank goodness you're okay."

"Of course I'm okay. You just left me. What's going on, Todd?"

"When I went back to your driveway to pick up my car, two of the tires were slashed, and there was a note attached to the windshield. It was addressed to you, warning you to drop the case."

"Did you call the police?" Anna asked.

"No. I ran straight here to make sure that you were okay. I'll do that now."

"I'll call Charlie," Velma said. "You two sit down."

Kathy placed the cup of water in front of Todd.

He took a shallow sip. "I'm okay. Let's meet Charlie at your house. We have to find out who did this. You could be in serious danger, Anna."

"So could you," Anna said.

"I don't think so. The note on my car was addressed to you. I think whoever left it thought my car was yours."

Anna had to smirk when she thought of Todd's shiny BMW. "The person must think my business is doing *really* well."

"Anna, how can you joke about this? Aren't you scared?" Todd asked.

"Nothing scares Anna," Velma said. "If whoever left the note is trying to get her to back off, it's a losing battle. It ain't gonna happen." Velma stepped away to call Charlie.

Todd looked wide-eyed at Anna. "I'm not sure whether to be impressed by your courage or concerned for your safety."

"Are you kidding? This kind of thing makes me even more determined to find Chester's killer. In a way, it's actually a good thing that it happened. It means we're on the right track. If we weren't, the killer wouldn't feel threatened."

"I suppose. But still, Anna. Maybe we should heed the warning and leave this to the police."

"I appreciate your concern, Todd. But Velma's right. I'm not going to back down now."

Velma returned. "Charlie wants the two of you to meet him at Anna's house. He's leaving the station right now."

By the time Anna and Todd got back to Anna's, Charlie was already there with another police officer. "Let me guess. You're investigating Chester's death, and the killer isn't happy about it."

"That seems to be the case," Anna said. "No pun intended."

"One of these days I'm going to be leading a murder investigation where you weren't there when the victim was killed."

"That sounds like a good plan to me," Anna said.

Charlie motioned for Todd and Anna to follow him to Anna's porch, where they all sat down. "Tell me everything."

Anna turned to Todd. "Todd is the one who found the note and had his tires slashed."

"But I think the person thought my car was Anna's, because the note was addressed to Anna. We had just talked to Oliver…"

"Wait. You suspect that Oliver Corbyn is the killer?" Charlie asked.

"No. He was on vacation with his family and has an alibi. We just thought he could shed some light on a few things."

"Anyway," Todd continued, "we had coffee afterwards to discuss the case. When I returned to Anna's house to get my car, this typewritten note was on the windshield, and two of my tires were slashed."

"I see," Charlie said, putting on gloves and taking the note. He slipped it into a plastic bag. "We'll check it for fingerprints, but I'm guessing we won't find any."

The other police officer, who Charlie had introduced as Officer Day, came over and joined them. Whoever did this didn't seem to leave any clues behind, but I'll talk to the neighbors and see if anyone saw anything."

"There's no need for the two of you to hang around," Charlie said. "Just be careful. Both of you."

"I'd better call a tow service. I only have one spare tire in my trunk, and I have two that need to be replaced."

"I'll wait with you," Anna said.

Within a half hour, Todd and his car were off to the nearest garage, and Charlie and Officer Day were finished talking to the neighbors, so Anna went back to work.

Later that afternoon, Todd came back to *Bella's Dream*. He

ordered an ice cream cone, and Anna gave it to him on the house. "I feel like I'm always giving you free ice cream to thank you for something," Anna said.

Todd smiled. "I'll take it. But I didn't come for free ice cream. After I got my car fixed, I went back to Oliver's and told him what happened. It turns out that after we left, Oliver called Nick and Drake and told them that he had talked to us. He said he felt guilty for suspecting his father and brother of murder, so he called out of respect to give them the courtesy of knowing he spoke to us."

"That means that Nick and Drake know that we're not giving up. If either of them is the killer, Oliver's call could have angered them, and perhaps one of them slashed your tires while we were having coffee."

"It's possible," Todd said. "I also called Allie and Jackson. I thought they should know what happened. They are on their way over here now."

CHAPTER 22

*a*llie and Jackson arrived at *Bella's Dream* within a few minutes. They had both been at work, but they left immediately after receiving Todd's text.

"Anna, this has gone too far," Allie said. "Jackson and I appreciate all that the two of you have done to help bring Uncle Chester's killer to justice, but we insist that you stop. This has become dangerous. Whoever did this already killed one person, and we have no reason to believe he or she won't strike again."

Todd looked intently at Anna. "I'm fairly certain that no matter what you say, you are not going to convince Anna to stop investigating."

Anna detected fear in Todd's gaze. She wasn't sure if he was afraid for his own safety or for hers.

"I'll be honest with you, Todd's right. I refuse to let a killer dictate my actions."

"I understand where you're coming from," Allie said. "But your safety is at risk. Think of how we would feel if anything happened to you. One tragedy connected to our anniversary party is more than enough."

Anna felt a surge of defensiveness. Their concern was both touching and intrusive at the same time. "I need you all to understand first of all, that I can take care of myself. And second, that if anything did happen to me, it would be the result of my own choice. It's not your fault that someone killed Chester, and it wasn't your decision for me to get involved."

That seemed to placate Allie and Jackson, but Todd still seemed a bit agitated.

"Of course, I'm just speaking for myself. Todd, you don't have to continue with the case. I would completely understand if you stepped back. You've already done so much, both by assisting me at the hot fudge sundae bar and helping me with the case."

"I'd be lying if I said I was fearless, but I'm in this as long as you are, Anna. I guess your resolve is contagious." The fear in his eyes faded.

"Okay, then." Anna gestured toward a booth in the back of the dining room, where they were sure to have some privacy. "Why don't we sit down and decide what to do next, unless the two of you need to get back to work."

"I'm okay for a little while longer," Allie said.

"Me, too," Jackson said.

Anna and Todd relayed to Allie and Jackson what they learned talking to Oliver. They told them how, even though Drake seemed to be acting cocky lately, Oliver didn't believe his brother or father was capable of murder.

"I tend to agree. But then again, I didn't think anyone who

was at our party was capable of murder, but *someone* obviously was," Jackson said.

"We did learn something interesting, though," Todd said. "Eliza told us she accepted a job with another company after Chester's death, but Oliver knows someone who works for that company, and Eliza accepted the job *before* Chester was killed. She is due to start the new job at the first of the year, after the current secretary retires."

"I just had a thought," Anna said. "We only have Eliza's word that Drake broke into Chester's office. If she's the killer, she could be lying about that, too. Under the circumstances, we don't know if we can trust her."

"That's a good point," Todd said.

"I hate to admit it, but I really hope it's not Nick or Drake. I would be crushed if it was a member of the family. Not that I want it to be Eliza or Dorothea, but..."

Jackson finished her sentence. "It would be an easier pill to swallow."

"Does that make me a horrible person?" Allie asked.

Jackson shook his head. "This is an awful situation. I'm just looking forward to the day when the killer is behind bars, and we can all begin to move forward from this mess."

"We should talk to Drake next," Todd said. "We need to find out for sure whether he was in Chester's office. Of course, he could deny it even if he was, but if he does confirm it, we'll know Eliza was telling the truth."

"I hope Drake didn't do it, too," Jackson said. "But I have to admit that I agree with Oliver. Drake had been acting really cocky lately. I know Allie doesn't want to admit it, but we talked about it even before Chester's death. I think we have to consider the possibility that Drake or Nick did this. Or even that they might have done it together. Between the two of them, there are several reasons why Chester's death could benefit them."

"Do either of you have any sense which way the police are leaning?" Anna asked Allie and Jackson. "I don't dare ask Charlie. It's bad enough he knows we are investigating after today."

"Charlie calls regularly with an update, but it doesn't sound like they are close to arresting anyone," Allie said. "He did say that there were no fingerprints on the jar that contained the poisoned hot fudge, which isn't surprising. Beyond that, the police haven't told us much. Charlie simply assures us that they are doing everything they can to find the killer."

"Then we all agree," Anna said. "Our next step is to talk to Drake and Nick again."

The others nodded.

"We'll need more of a plan than that," Todd said. "If we just go there and question them, they'll deny everything. We need a strategy."

"You're right," Anna said. "We're all tired. It's been a stressful morning, and we all need to get back to work. Why don't we give it some thought and regroup today or tomorrow?"

They all agreed, and everyone left *Bella's Dream*, except for Anna.

"How's it going?" Velma asked, when Anna rejoined her behind the ice cream counter.

"We decided to give ourselves a little time to come up with a strategy."

"You look like you could use a break. I think this is taking more of a toll on you than you care to admit," Velma said.

Velma was partly right. It was actually her search for Bella that was taking a toll on Anna. Every trip to Maine dashed her hopes a little, no matter how much she tried not to let it. But she let Velma believe that it was Chester's case. "I guess you're right. I'm not going to stop investigating because of what happened, but it does have me a little jumpy. It's never fun to have your life threatened." At least that wasn't a complete lie.

"Why don't you get away from the store for a little while?" Velma suggested.

"That's a good idea. Maybe I'll take a walk."

Anna found herself wandering into *The Book Cove*, the bookstore that her friend Ruthie owned. Ruthie immediately came over to greet her.

"It's good to see you Anna," Ruthie said, giving her a hug. "How's business going?"

"Not as slow as I was afraid it would be this time of year. So far, I'm managing to keep everything going and pay everyone's salaries, including my own, without drawing on any of my savings from the summer. I can't ask for more than that during the off season."

"It should be this way through Christmas," Ruthie said. "The town's Christmas festivities keep people on Main Street until then. But for a few months after that, don't be surprised if you have to dip into the summer's profits to pay everyone's salaries."

"I'm going to have to be especially creative at bringing customers in during those months. Before Thanksgiving, I'm going to plan some events so that we can hit the ground running with a full entertainment schedule come January."

"You mean, events like the hot fudge sundae bar where murders take place? I swear you could do a mystery-themed night."

Anna chuckled. "A mystery-themed night would be a blast. But I think it would hit too close to home. People might think I was making light of the recent murders in Seagull Cove."

"Fair point," Ruthie said.

"So, you put it together that I was running the hot fudge sundae bar when Chester was murdered."

"I did. But only because I know you. I had my suspicions, so I asked Jeremy Russo when he came in the other day."

"How's your poetry book coming?" Anna asked.

"It's getting a final copyedit now, and I'll be publishing it by Thanksgiving." Ruthie pulled her phone from her pocket and handed it to Anna. "I just got my cover design back. What do you think?"

The cover file contained a tasteful artistic rendering of the cove, dotted with people of all ages. The inn sat on a rocky cliff behind a flock of seagulls gliding through a blue sky.

"It's beautiful, Ruthie. Congratulations! Don't forget to drop off some copies at my shop so I can put them up for sale."

"I'll definitely do that."

"Speaking of local authors, did you know the nephew of the victim is an author?" Ruthie asked.

"I did. I heard his second book just came out."

"It came out last week." Ruthie walked Anna to a table of new releases and there was Drake's book, front and center, beneath a sign that read, 'local author.' "I'm giving it some extra publicity since Drake Corbyn is a local."

Anna flipped through the book. It was a psychological

thriller. "I think I'll take a copy," Anna said. "I'm all for supporting local talent."

A knowing smirk spread across Ruthie's face. "Wait a minute. I know you too well, Anna McBride." Then she looked around, apparently to be sure she couldn't be overheard, and lowered her voice. "Drake Corbyn is one of your suspects, isn't he? I'll bet you're buying this book to try to get a better idea of how his mind works."

Anna had to laugh. "I'm not even going to try to deny that. Who knows? Maybe it will help. Besides, it's a win-win. If he didn't do it, then I'll legitimately be happy to support a local author."

"Good luck," Ruthie said, after ringing up Anna's purchase.

When Anna returned to *Bella's Dream*, Joe Wiggins was in his usual seat at the counter.

"How goes the investigation?"

Anna was surprised to hear Joe ask about the investigation until she realized he was referring to Bella.

"It's going." Anna caught him up on her two trips to Maine without Jeremy and how she hit dead ends both times. "Jeremy and I are going again on Thursday. I'm trying to stay positive, but we're already halfway through the list."

"Hang in there. Nobody ever said sleuthing was glamorous."

"It's anything *but* glamorous. It's time-consuming, and there are far more disappointments than leads." But Anna would make a thousand trips to Maine if it meant talking to Bella even one more time.

"You're always welcome to join us, Joe." Anna didn't want him to think she ditched him now that she had an additional partner in crime.

"That's okay. I'm getting too old for grunt work, and I'd be a third wheel with your cover story. But keep me posted, and if you don't find her in one of the salons on the list I gave you, I'll help you figure out another plan."

"Thanks, Joe. I appreciate all that you do."

He winked. "I know, kiddo."

Since business was slow, Anna decided to leave work early. She was curious about what was in that book of Drake's, so she decided to spend a quiet evening at home reading.

CHAPTER 23

After heating some leftovers for supper, Anna put a log in the fireplace, warmed some apple cider, and curled up on her couch in a soft hunter green sweatshirt and yoga pants. She took Drake's book from its bag and began reading.

Anna read the first chapter and was pleasantly surprised. It was a gripping, fast-paced book with loads of unexpected twists and turns. She couldn't put it down.

At midnight, she was still engrossed in the book. Drake was a fantastic writer. Anna began to feel a twinge of compassion for him for not being able to pursue his dream when he was so talented. But then again, Oliver was right. Drake should never have let Chester control his life. It was his own fault for being greedy. Drake should have pursued his passion and let the chips fall where they may.

As the evening wore on, Anna tried to stay awake, but her heavy eyes betrayed her. She did her best to fight the urge to go to bed.

Just one more chapter.

As Anna continued reading, she began to notice some interesting things about the book's antagonist, Bart. Bart was a wealthy investor who was also a controlling and difficult man. He manipulated his family and made the lives of his loved ones difficult because of his short-tempered nature. But it wasn't until Bart's family and friends became angry at him for convincing them to invest in a real estate project without doing sufficient research that Anna realized the extent of the similarities between Bart and Chester. Bart's family and friends were furious with him for being so careless with their money. As a result, a couple of the other characters began plotting their revenge – in the form of murder.

This was no coincidence. Anna was certain of it. When Drake wrote his book, he didn't know about Chester's health issues. If he were modeling the character of Bart off Chester, which he seemingly was, Drake believed that like Bart, Chester had simply been negligent with their money. And his friends and family were plotting their revenge.

Suddenly, Anna was wide awake. She reread the previous chapter, paying close attention to every detail. Everything she knew about Chester's bad investment was right there on the page. Drake had used the situation verbatim in his book.

Did Drake break into Chester's office because he was looking for details about the investment so he could use it in one of his books? Or was it for the purpose of plotting his own revenge for what Chester had done to his father, gaining a sizeable inheritance for them both in the process?

Anna looked at the alarm clock on her nightstand. It was well past midnight. She wouldn't be able to tell Todd or Allie and Jackson about Drake's book until the morning. She did her best to sleep but ended up tossing and turning all night. Finally, at 8:00, still tired from her late night, she dragged herself out of bed.

She showered, had breakfast, and when it seemed like a respectable hour, she called Todd to tell him what she discovered.

"Let me get this straight," Todd said. "Drake worked Chester's bad investment into his *book*?"

"He included every last detail we learned from Dorothea and Eliza and then some."

"It sounds like we need to talk to Drake as soon as possible and see what he has to say. I have a few time-sensitive phone calls that I need to make this morning, but my afternoon is flexible."

"Perfect. I'll call Allie and Jackson and fill them in. Maybe they'll know where we can find Drake this afternoon."

As soon as she hung up with Todd, Anna called Allie and told her what she discovered about Drake's book.

"That's crazy," Allie said. "With everything that has happened in the past ten days, I haven't had a chance to read Drake's latest release. Are you *sure* that's what he did? Maybe it was just a coincidence."

"There are far too many similarities," Anna said. "I was hoping you would know where Todd and I could find him today. We want to talk to him right away."

"I'll try to arrange something for tonight," Allie said. "This is one interview I want to be present for. I need some answers from my cousin, and I want to hear them straight from his own mouth."

"Okay. Call me when you've arranged something."

Anna spent the morning at *Bella's Dream*. Just before lunch, her cell phone rang, and Allie's name popped onto her screen.

"Hi, Allie."

"Hi, Anna. I arranged for Drake to come over to my house after dinner tonight. Can you and Todd come around 7:00?"

"We'll be there. Does Drake know why we want to talk to him?"

"I told him you were coming and that a few more questions came up about the investigation. I didn't want to ambush him, but I also didn't want to give him too much information. I thought it was best not to give him time to come up with any stories."

"Nice job," Anna said. "I'll see you tonight."

Anna texted Todd, and he offered to pick her up at *Bella's Dream* shortly before 7:00, so they could go together.

About 5:00, Anna needed a change of scenery, so she went to the *Sand Dollar Grille* and ordered a club sandwich and sweet potato fries. She took her time eating, then walked back to *Bella's Dream* to wait for Todd. She was still tired from reading late into the night, so she brewed some strong coffee and drank it while she waited.

Todd arrived right on time, and shortly after, they were sitting in Allie's and Jackson's living room with the young couple and Drake - in the same room where Chester had died just ten days before.

"As I told Allie," Drake said, "I can't imagine what else I could tell you that I haven't already told both you and the police."

"We had a couple of questions concerning your book."

Drake's shoulders relaxed. "Oh, Allie said it was about the investigation. I'm always happy to talk about my book, especially now that I don't have to keep my author career a secret."

"I was at *The Book Cove* yesterday and was talking to the owner, Ruthie. I understand you'll be doing a book signing there this month."

Drake beamed proudly. "That's right. It's always fun to do a book signing in your hometown."

"I also picked up a copy of your book while I was there. I must admit, it was quite good. I was up reading well into the night. I got all the way to chapter fifteen."

The proud smile Drake was wearing quickly faded. "Oh, I think I understand where this conversation is going."

"Anna told me that one of the characters in your book bore a striking resemblance to Uncle Chester. I have to admit, it's a bit disturbing," Allie said.

"So, what's the big deal? I turned Uncle Chester into a character in one of my books. While I was writing it, I found out from my father that Uncle Chester caused a lot of good people to lose money, including his own brother, because of his carelessness. At least that's what we thought at the time. We didn't know about his illness. When my father first told me about the investment, I was horrified, but once I settled down, I realized it sounded exactly like the kind of thing the book's antagonist, Bart, would do. I hadn't realized it at the time, but I guess I gave a bunch of Uncle's Chester's character traits to Bart. There's no harm done. Nobody but the family will know what I did. The man certainly caused my father and me enough grief over the years. I figured he owed me. In a way, it was poetic justice. Uncle Chester helped me to write a book without knowing it after he had done so much to try to end my writing career before it even began. Even though it wasn't his fault in the end, he still wasted my father's money. This way, Uncle Chester's mistake helps our family earn some of my father's money back through my book sales. I don't see the big deal."

"The big deal is that the antagonist in your book ends up being poisoned to death," Allie said. "And that's exactly what happened to our uncle."

"Oh, come on, Allie. If I were planning on killing Uncle Chester, do you honestly think I would have signaled it to the world, not to mention the police, by writing about it first?"

Drake did bring up a solid point.

"At least now you know why I broke into the office. If I were going to kill him over that, I wouldn't have needed to break in. I already had all the information I needed to have my motive."

"So, you broke in because you were looking for details for your story," Jackson said.

"Exactly. When Eliza caught me taking photos of the documents, I knew she would see, if she didn't already know, that my father was one of the investors. I figured she'd assume I was trying to get information on his behalf. Only close family knew about my books, so I didn't want to tell her my real reason for being there. She worked too closely with Uncle Chester. It would have put her in an awkward situation if I told her what I was really doing."

Maybe Drake was telling the truth. It did explain a lot - his cocky attitude toward Chester that Allie, Jackson, and Oliver had picked up on, and his snooping around his uncle's office.

"Look, let me put it this way. If I were going to kill Uncle Chester, I would have at least changed up some of the details in my book. I had no way of knowing Uncle Chester would be murdered. It was just a horrible coincidence – even down to the fact that he was murdered by poison. As much as I despised the man at times, he was my uncle, and nobody deserved to die like that."

CHAPTER 24

"So, did you learn anything interesting about the investment when you were looking through your uncle's file?" Todd asked Drake.

"I just saw that he purchased the property without first checking to see if the land was buildable for the kind of project that he had in mind. The list of investors showed that most of them were family and friends. It made sense, because they are the only ones who would trust my uncle enough to invest without doing their research. They all assumed that Uncle Chester had already done his due diligence. I'll admit that I was angry, because it *did* look like negligence. I believed that what I learned confirmed my suspicions about my uncle being careless with good peoples' hard-earned money. But on the other hand, it was confusing, because it wasn't like him to treat investors poorly. I guess I let myself assume that he was getting more selfish as he got older. Now that we know that his brain tumor was affecting his judgement, it makes a lot more sense. But I can assure you, even when I was the angriest at him, it never crossed my mind to kill him over it.

And if it had, I wouldn't have included it in a book. That would have been dumb."

"Did your father know you were using all this as part of your plot?"

"Not until the book came out. But we both got a good chuckle out of it. I knew he would appreciate the irony of Uncle Chester supporting my career, despite his best efforts to squash it."

Jackson shook his head and smiled. "You know, if Chester hadn't died, it really would have been funny."

"Now that more time has gone by since Chester's death, have you had any more ideas as to who might have done it?" Anna asked.

Drake seemed relieved to have the focus off himself. He smirked as if he were about to divulge a juicy piece of gossip.

"There *was* something else I discovered while going through the files in Chester's office. Eliza has a secret."

"What kind of secret?" Anna asked.

"While I was searching for the file on the investment, I discovered another file with a red tab. I opened it, and it contained Eliza's resume. Someone had drawn a circle around the section about her education and put a question mark next to it. I skimmed right past it, since it wasn't what I was looking for. But a few days ago, I asked Aunt Violet what it was all about."

"What did she say?"

"It turns out that when Uncle Chester hired Eliza, she put on her resume that she had a Bachelor's degree from Boston College. After he hired her, she said something that led Uncle Chester to believe she may not have gone to college at all. According to Aunt Violet, he became suspicious, because Eliza didn't know what a syllabus was. Apparently, Uncle Chester did some research and discovered that Eliza hadn't in fact attended Boston College. Or any college, for that matter. She lied on her resume."

"He obviously didn't fire her over it. How would that have given Eliza a motive to kill him?"

"According to Aunt Violet, he always held it over her and used it to make her feel indebted to him. Once, when she tried to give her notice, he threatened that if anyone called for a recommendation, he would tell them that she forged her education on her resume. He didn't want her to leave, and in true Uncle Chester style, he did whatever he needed to ensure that he got his way."

"Is she that good of a secretary?" Todd asked.

Drake shrugged his shoulders. "She's good, but I think it was more of a control issue. He was like that. Sometimes I think he just got a rush out of controlling people. Aunt Violet says that he got worse after he lost his sister. Personally, I just think he was mean."

"We knew Chester was making it difficult for Eliza to leave, but we didn't know he was blackmailing her," Todd said.

"In your opinion, Drake, did Eliza want her freedom enough to kill for it?" Anna asked.

"Aunt Violet doesn't think so. But who knows. That man was difficult, and she was with him forty hours per week. If I were in her shoes, I'd be anxious to leave."

When they finished talking to Drake, Todd drove Anna home. "I don't think Drake did it," he said.

"I tend to agree. It's not that he doesn't have as strong a motive as everyone else we talked to, but I just can't imagine that he would be so stupid as to commit murder after writing about it in a book so that everyone could trace it back to him."

"That would be pretty dumb," Todd said.

"Okay. He's off our list of suspects."

"We're down to Eliza, Dorothea, and Nick."

"At least we're narrowing in on the killer," Anna said. "I have a busy day tomorrow. How about if we take tomorrow off, and get back to it on Friday?"

"Sounds good to me. Since we want to talk to Dorothea again, should we meet at Mile Long Beach for another early morning walk on Friday? We could also go back to Chester's office to talk to Eliza after Dorothea."

"We'll definitely need to talk to Eliza on Friday," Anna said. "Eliza said she would only be working at Chester's office for two weeks to close out his accounts, which means that Friday will be her last day."

"All right. I'll meet you at Mile Long Beach bright and early on Friday morning," Todd said.

After Todd drove away, Anna didn't go inside her cottage. There was something she had been meaning to do. She wanted to know for sure if Chester's brain tumor could have affected his judgement to such a degree, and there was only one doctor in town who she knew well enough to ask.

Anna made a quick stop at *Bella's Dream* to pick up a pint of rocky road ice cream, Daniel's favorite flavor, and walked to his Victorian house across the street from Mile Long Beach.

"Anna, what a pleasant surprise!" Daniel said when he opened the door and saw Anna on the other side.

"I come bearing gifts." Anna handed him the container of rocky road.

"You remembered my favorite flavor."

"I have a freakishly good memory when it comes to ice cream. Now, ask me what I had for breakfast, and I might not be able to tell you."

Daniel chuckled and invited Anna inside. "Wanda tells me that she told you about our son, Danny."

Anna nodded. "Yes. I'm so sorry for what happened to Danny."

Daniel nodded.

"Wanda must like you. She very rarely talks about what happened, and I don't think she's ever told anyone why we're separated. Can I get you a scoop?" he offered, holding up the container.

"No thanks. I already eat more than I should at work."

Daniel put the ice cream in the freezer. "I can imagine. I would have no willpower if I worked in an ice cream shop. Did you come to ask about Danny?"

"Oh, no, my visit has nothing to do with that, although I *am* happy that Wanda opened up to me. I've liked her from the moment we met. I couldn't ask for a better neighbor."

Daniel smiled. "I can't argue with that. There's something special about my wife. Then you just came to give me ice cream?"

"Well, not exactly. I had a question about something else that I thought you might be able to help me with, as a doctor."

Daniel's eyes widened. "Is everything okay, Anna?"

"Oh, yes, of course. It doesn't have anything to do with me."

He breathed a sigh of relief. "I'm glad to hear that."

"I was wondering if a brain tumor could cause someone to make decisions they never would have otherwise made - decisions that display a lack of judgment. And could such an illness cause somebody to be... How can I say this? More difficult to be around."

Daniel's demeanor transformed from that of a friendly neighbor into a thoughtful physician. "Well, it depends on a few things, such as the location of the tumor, but yes, that happens. In fact, it happens a lot. A person can become more irritable and short-tempered. They can become easily overwhelmed. And it can certainly affect someone's judgement. Do you know somebody who's sick?"

"Kind of. You may have heard about the recent murder in Seagull Cove."

"Yes. Chester Corbyn. He was a local businessman. I read that he was murdered at his niece's anniversary party. I remember thinking what a strange cause of death it was. Wait a minute! Was the murder connected with your shop in any way?"

Anna explained how she and Todd were at the party running a hot fudge sundae bar, and how they were now investigating. She explained how Chester had a brain tumor that nobody knew about, which had apparently affected his behavior. "According to his family and friends, Chester always had a difficult personality, but they said that it became worse over the past couple of months. His wife believed it was because of his illness, but I wanted to know for sure if that were possible. According to those who knew him best, he became more difficult to be around, and he'd been making some bad business decisions towards the end of his life."

"Ah, I see. Well, yes, that is not uncommon. His behavior could very well have been connected to the tumor. In addition, receiving a terminal diagnosis could have similar affects.

A person could become anxious and irritable trying to come to terms with news like that. It could have been a combination of both."

"Of course," Anna said. "That's a good point."

Daniel smiled warmly. "It sounds like you're involved in some dangerous work. Please be careful. I don't want to see anything happen to my wife's favorite neighbor."

Anna returned his smile. "Thank you, Daniel. I will. I'm so glad my cottage is next to Wanda's."

"She doesn't always express what she feels, but I can tell you with certainty that she feels the same way."

CHAPTER 25

*J*eremy picked Anna up in the late morning on Thursday for their daytrip to Maine to visit more salons.

Anna tucked Joe's trusted list into the front pocket of her jeans and hopped into Jeremy's car.

"I have a good feeling about today," he said.

"I'm glad to hear that. I didn't make much progress during my last two excursions, so I'm trying not to get my hopes up. After the salons we visit today, there are only a handful left on the list. I have no idea what I'll do next if this list turns out to be a dead end."

"We'll cross that bridge when we come to it. We haven't hit the end of the list yet. We still have today and at least one more trip after that. Everything can change in an instant."

That was true. After all, before Joe spotted Bella across the street, peering into her shop on the morning of the grand opening of *Bella's Dream*, Anna had no indication that Bella might still be alive.

"I appreciate your positivity, Jeremy. I could use the moral support today, not to mention the company. The next town on our list is Camden, which is three-and-a-half hours north of Seagull Cove. You really are a trooper for coming with me on this one."

He smiled at Anna.

They headed north on Route 95, following it to Route 295. November was quickly approaching, and while it was no longer peak foliage season that far north, the view out the car window as they drove was still breathtaking. It was late afternoon by the time they had arrived in Camden. Between Jeremy's optimism and the fact that they were the furthest from Seagull Cove than they had been while looking for Bella, Anna had allowed her hopes to rise by the time they arrived at the first of four salons they would visit that day. "Maybe we'll have more luck now that we're further north. After all, it makes sense that Bella would have gone as far away from Boston as possible to avoid being recognized."

"Here's to hoping you're right."

As they got out of the car, Anna's cell phone rang.

"It says, 'potential spam,'" Anna said. "I think I'll turn it off for now."

The first two salons they visited were a bust. Nobody had heard of Izzy, although the nail technicians they talked with confessed that they were new to the business.

Anna's heart sank. "Only two more to go. After today, the only salons left are way up north. It will take forever to get there." Her disappointment must have been obvious.

"I know it's tough to keep focused, but at this point, it's a mental game," Jeremy said. "Try to stay positive. If we need to, we can drive north on Sunday and stay the night in a hotel, so we can hit the ground running on Monday."

"Are you sure you want to do this all over again on Monday? You must have better things to do on your days off than traipsing around Maine with me."

"I'm almost as determined to get through this list as you are, Anna. At least we will know one way or another by then whether Bella ever worked at any of these salons. And for the record, I can't think of anything more important to be doing than this."

Anna gave him a grateful smile.

"You look tired," Jeremy said.

"To be honest, I had so much on my mind this morning that I didn't eat much."

"Why don't we stop and get you a sandwich before we hit the last two salons? No matter how things go at our last two stops, it won't do you any good to be hungry."

"That's probably a wise idea."

They stopped at a small sandwich shop that boasted farm-to-table ingredients. Anna ordered a tomato, basil, and mozzarella sandwich on focaccia bread along with a hot chocolate to lift her spirits. Jeremy convinced her to add some whipped cream.

Jeremy got a cinnamon roll that looked to be the size of a small child's head, and a hot apple cider. They enjoyed their food at a bistro table by a large picture window.

"This was a good suggestion," Anna said. "I feel much better now."

On their way out, they got two coffees to go to further boost their energy for their remaining stops and for the long drive home. Then they drove to the next salon.

There were two nail technicians giving manicures and a

middle-aged woman with straight bleached red hair giving a client a pedicure.

The woman with red hair looked up. "Can I book the two of you for a couples' service?"

They both shook their head.

"We're here because we are looking for someone." Anna gave their usual spiel about trying to locate a high school classmate for an upcoming reunion.

"You don't have a last name?" the woman asked.

"We know her maiden name, but we heard she got married, and nobody seem to have her married name," Jeremy said. "But her first name is Isabel. She goes by Izzy."

Anna described Bella to the woman. "At least that's what she looked like five years ago, when one of our friends saw her last," Anna said.

The woman thought hard. "Nobody by that name has ever worked here, but it does sound familiar."

Anna and Todd looked at one another with what Anna hoped wasn't an overly excited expression.

"Could she work at another salon nearby?" Anna asked.

"It's possible. Come to think of it, I think she may have worked at *Phenomenail Salon*." The woman put the emphasis on the last syllable of the first word. "I'm not sure, mind you, but I would check there."

"That's the next salon on our list," Anna said. "Thank you so much!"

Anna held in a squeal until they got inside the car. "I'm trying not to get my hopes up, since she wasn't certain, but Bella might be living and working a short distance from where we are right now!"

Anna took a deep breath and said a silent prayer as Jeremy

started the car. She plugged the address of the next salon into her GPS and they headed to *Phenomenail*.

Anna took another deep breath and slowly got out of the car. She wanted to savor the excitement she was feeling in case it turned out to be another dead end.

"Do you know what you'll say if you see her?"

Anna shook her head. "I'm hoping the words will just come." She peeked in the window before walking in the front door, and Jeremy walked up behind her. "I don't see Bella in there now."

"She could be out back, or it could be her day off."

Anna pushed open the glass door. A young woman was sitting on a couch in the back, tapping away on her phone. She looked up. "I'll be right with you."

"Sorry about that," the young woman said when she arrived at the front desk. "Some clients like to make their appointments via text. I was just confirming one for tomorrow."

"That's not a problem," Anna said, proceeding to give the woman their story about looking for an old classmate.

"Nobody by the name of Izzy works here now, but hold on. Let me get Bertha."

Anna's heart once again sank. She had allowed herself to hope that she might see Bella that afternoon.

The young woman disappeared for a moment and returned with an older heavyset woman.

"Hi, I'm Bertha. I hear you're looking for a technician named Izzy?"

"Yes." Anna quickly recounted their fabricated story. "She has red hair and a great sense of humor."

"I just bought this spa about a year ago and only a couple

of the technicians stayed on when the spa changed owners. But I do remember a red-headed nail technician named Izzy. She was a lovely woman. I gave all the technicians who worked for the previous owner the opportunity to stay on before hiring new staff. Izzy personally paid me a visit to inform me that she was choosing to leave not because of anything against me, but because she was looking for a change. If I remember correctly, she had just been hired for a job working for an assisted living facility. They were looking to hire a nail technician to service their residents. Izzy said that she wanted to try serving a different population."

That *did* sound like something Bella would do.

"Do you know which facility?" Anna asked.

"There aren't many in the area. It has to be *Camden Manor*. They are a rehabilitation center, assisted living, and nursing home facility all on one campus. It's about fifteen minutes from here. They are the only place big enough to hire their own technician."

"Thank you," Anna said. "We'll see if she's there. One more question," Anna said, pulling her phone from her pocket and quickly scrolling to a photo of Bella. "I just want to be sure we're talking about the same person. Is this the Izzy that you are talking about?"

"Yup, that's her. Her hair is shorter now, but that's Izzy."

Anna couldn't stop the smile from reaching both ears, no matter how hard she tried to play it cool. "Thank you so much! You've been extremely helpful!"

CHAPTER 26

When they got back into the car, it took a minute before Anna was able to speak. "Did I hear her right? Did Bella actually work in this salon up until last year? I just can't believe it! My ears must be betraying me."

Jeremy's smile matched the joy Anna felt inside. He wrapped his hand around hers and squeezed it. "You heard right. I'm so happy for you, Anna."

As if having the same thought at the same time, they both glanced at the dashboard.

"It's nearly 5:00," Jeremy said. "What do you want to do next?"

Anna leaned back in the seat. "My instinct is to immediately drive over to the assisted living facility, but it'll be after 5:00 by the time we get there, so there is little chance that she'd be working now."

"That's a good point. Now that we know where she works, we don't want to alert her to the fact that you're looking for her and give her the chance to flee."

"As hard as it is to not go racing over, I should come back

another time. It will give me a chance to give some thought to a plan and run it by Joe."

"I agree," Jeremy said. "That's the best way to handle it. When we were looking for her in one of the salons on Joe's list, we had no choice but to take our chances that someone could alert her that we were searching for her. But now that we have some solid intel about where she works, you should do this right. The last thing you want to do is to scare her away."

"It's settled then. Let's drive back. I'll talk to Joe, and we'll come back when we have a solid plan," Anna said.

As they drove back to Seagull Cove, Anna was lost in thought. Now she knew beyond a shadow of a doubt that Bella was alive. However, as excited as she was that they had found their most promising lead yet and that she may be very close to seeing her sister again, Anna found herself growing nervous along with her excitement. The magnitude of what was happening was sinking in. How would Bella react to seeing her? Would she have changed as a result of the years gone by and whatever she had lived through? Bella could even be married or have children by now, for all Anna knew.

What felt like a few minutes later, but in reality was three-and-a-half hours later, Jeremy dropped Anna off at her cottage.

"Sorry I've been so quiet on the drive home. It was a long drive, and I wasn't much of a conversationalist," Anna said.

"You have nothing to apologize for. You have a lot to process. Are you going to try to talk to Joe tonight?"

"No. I need to sit with this and think about it some more. Besides, I'm exhausted from the long car ride, and I want my mind to be sharp when I talk to him. I'll wait until he comes into my shop tomorrow. Then, I'll pull him aside for a nice, long chat."

"Keep me posted. Call me when you have a plan or if you need another sounding board while you formulate one."

"Will do, Jeremy," Anna said, pulling him into a hug. "Thank you so much for everything."

It was well past dinnertime. Anna took a quick walk over to *Bella's Dream* to check in on her staff, but since it was a slow evening, and nearly closing time, she headed back home and made herself a late dinner.

While Anna was eating her chicken, potato, and broccoli, she remembered that she had turned off her phone before they entered the first salon. When she turned it back on, there were a couple of text messages from Todd and one from Allie.

They both asked if Anna could call them as soon as possible.

Todd sounded concerned in his second message, which was about an hour ago, so she called him first.

"Hi, Anna, I was a little worried when I didn't hear back from you. You always seem to respond quickly to my texts."

"I usually have my phone on, but today I turned it off. I took the day off and headed to Maine to take care of some personal business. I meant to turn it back on when I was finished, but I guess I forgot."

"They say it's a good idea to turn off your phone and disconnect once in a while." Todd chuckled. "But every time I try to do that, I nearly have a panic attack that a client might want to reach me, so I end up more stressed than if I had just kept it on. In any case, I happened to run into Allie today and told her that we planned to talk to Dorothea in the morning. Allie told me that Dorothea had a bad cold, so she won't likely be at the beach for her morning walk. I think we should still talk to Eliza, but there's no need to get up early."

"If I didn't know better, it sounds like you're becoming the North Shore's next amateur sleuth," Anna joked.

"No, thank you. After this one, I'm going to retire my sleuthing jersey. I just can't seem to stop thinking about the case."

"I haven't thought much about it today, but last night, I paid a visit to a friend who also happens to be a doctor. He confirmed that a brain tumor can indeed cause the type of bizarre behavior that Chester's family and friends were reporting."

"I'm not surprised to hear that," Todd said. "But I suppose it was good to get it confirmed. Something about Chester's story sounded familiar, and I couldn't place my finger on it. Then, just before I called you, I realized that I had a buddy whose father got Alzheimer's, and a similar thing happened. He made a few bad investments and misjudged some business deals, and his family lost a lot of money. Of course, once they realized what was going on, his wife and son took over the finances. But I think that can be a telltale sign that someone is sick."

"I suppose that makes sense," Anna said.

"How about if I pick you up at 10:00 tomorrow morning?" Todd asked. "After I ran into Allie and heard about Dorothea, one of my biggest clients in Seagull Cove called and asked if I could meet with him in the morning, so I told him I could. We're meeting at 9:00."

"That sounds good," Anna said. "I'll see you at 10."

Anna was up late thinking about what happened in Maine, until she finally dozed off after midnight. Between thinking of their conversation with Eliza the following morning and her talk with Joe in the afternoon about Bella, she tossed and turned all night long.

Even though she could sleep in, since Todd wasn't coming until 10:00, Anna woke up early and couldn't get back to sleep. She hopped in the shower and had breakfast on her front porch. It was cool, but the sun was already shining, and the fresh air felt nice.

About halfway through breakfast, Casper came wandering up her street from the direction of Main Street. "I know my employees have been feeding you. Are you here to tell me that you've missed me?"

Casper brushed against her legs.

Anna went inside to open a can of tuna and put it out in an old bowl that she recently set aside for Casper's use. She was glad to have the company.

She scratched the top of his head as she placed the food in front of him. "You must be getting desperate, little guy. Are fewer of the Main Street business owners remembering to feed you now that the weather is cooling down? Is that why you're coming to my house? Or do you just miss me?"

Anna smiled. The way Casper was devouring his tuna, she could guess his answer to that question.

"How about a little conversation over breakfast, Casper? Who do you think killed Chester?" She wondered if Casper would come to her home more frequently as it got colder. She had heard that some of the Main Street shops close for the month of January. What would he do for food? She had a feeling he was resourceful enough to survive, and he had obviously made it through past winters, but nonetheless, Anna made a mental note to remember to look out for him.

After all, desperation could make a feral cat do strange things. And food would only become scarcer as the days grew colder and darker.

Wait, that's it! Things would only get worse than they were now. And that wasn't only true for cats in challenging situations. It could be true for humans, as well.

Anna couldn't believe she hadn't thought of that before. She and Todd needed to talk to Eliza. ASAP.

CHAPTER 27

*A*nna started to text Todd to tell him that she just had an insight that might be the key to solving the case. But when she pulled her cell phone from her pocket, she saw that it was 9:30. He was probably in the middle of his meeting, so there was no point in disturbing him. He would be there soon enough.

When Casper finished his breakfast, he looked up at Anna. She couldn't help but smile at what she believed was gratitude. "You're welcome, little friend."

Then he scooted off in the direction of Main Street.

Anna washed Casper's dish and tried to busy herself in the yard while she waited for Todd to arrive. She raked a few more leaves, filling half a bag. When Todd still hadn't arrived by 10:10, she thought of calling. He was usually punctual, but she decided to give it a few more minutes, since she knew he was with a client. His meeting was probably running long. Anna did, however, text Velma to let her know she would be late to work. With their late start, they likely wouldn't be finished talking to Eliza by the time the shop opened.

Finally, at 10:20, Anna's phone rang.

"I'm so sorry, Anna, but I got tied up with work. Could we push our meeting back an hour?"

Shoot. Anna was ready to get this done. She was tempted to go alone, but she didn't know how things would unfold, so she decided to wait. "Sure."

"Great. You're the best. I'll see you soon."

Anna did some more raking until Todd pulled into her driveway at 11:15. She quickly grabbed her purse and ran down the porch steps before Todd could get out of his car.

"I'm sorry I'm late," he said. "It took longer with my client than I expected. He's one of my biggest clients, so I couldn't rush him along."

"No problem. But I'm about ready to jump out of my skin. I think I might know who killed Chester." It was a bittersweet realization. That is, if Anna was right.

"What?!"

"It's just a hunch. I should know more after we talk to Eliza."

They arrived at Chester's office within ten minutes. Eliza didn't look surprised to see them. "If it isn't the dynamic duo. I had a feeling I'd see the two of you again."

"Why is that?" Todd asked, narrowing his brow.

"It's been nearly two weeks, and the police haven't solved the case yet. I remember how determined you seemed when we last spoke."

Todd was eyeing Eliza suspiciously, but Anna kept the conversation moving forward. "We know it's your last day working here, and you must be busy. But we just had a couple of questions that we hoped you could answer for us."

Eliza shrugged her shoulders. "Why not? I'm actually not

too busy today. I've pretty much wrapped up all the loose ends. In fact, I expect to leave early."

Eliza led Anna and Todd to the waiting area where they had talked the last time they were in the office.

"What can I help you with?"

"We heard you accepted a job and that you're starting right after the first of the year," Todd said.

"Yes. I think I told you the last time you were here that I accepted a new job."

"But you didn't tell us that you accepted it *before* Chester was killed. Or that he was blackmailing you into staying," Todd said.

Her eyes widened.

Anna had a feeling that Todd believed that she thought Eliza was the killer. She should have told him to follow her lead. His accusatory tone was counterproductive.

"That's okay. You don't have to answer that," Anna said.

Todd gave Anna a confused glance.

"What I'd really like to know is what you have been working on here the past couple of weeks, since Chester died."

"That's a strange question. I don't see what it has to do with his murder."

"It may not have anything to do with it, but it might."

"Well, to be honest, there hasn't been a whole lot to do this week. I closed out most of Chester's affairs last week. Most of Chester's projects were in the acquisition and beginning phases. I informed those he was working with of his death and that his business would be closing. There were a few investment projects that Chester was trying to get off the ground. He had been looking for investors, so I called all of them, as well, to let them know those deals were off."

"Tell us more about his current projects. We heard that the real estate investment that Nick and Dorothea were involved in wasn't his only bad investment. Were a lot of them losing money?"

She let out a deep breath. "Yes. The few projects that he did have in the works were losing money. Luckily, most of them didn't have investors involved. He really did make some bad choices. I hadn't realized the extent of it until I went through his active files. I do secretarial work, so I'm not always privy to the finances. But Violet gave me access to all the files, so I could notify all the parties involved."

"And you said that most of that work was completed last week?" Anna asked.

"That's right. It didn't take as much time as I thought it might. Of course, some of the conversations were longer, because people had heard what happened and were either genuinely concerned or they wanted to gossip. Between the phone calls, some paperwork, and the funeral services, that took up the first week."

"What about this week?" Anna asked. "Was there anything for you to do?"

"This week I sent out some checks at Violet's request. She gave me a list of people who had lost money in Chester's recent investments. She asked me to call them on her behalf to ask how much they lost and to inform them that Violet intended to repay them. So, I made a spreadsheet with everyone's name, address, the investment they were involved in, and how much they had lost."

"Did you find that strange?" Anna asked. "Legally, she didn't have to do that."

"Yes and no. Violet has a huge heart, and it weighed heavily on her that so many good people lost a lot of money because they trusted Chester's business instincts."

"How many people were on the list?"

"Seven," Eliza said. "I showed her the list a few days ago. She signed the checks and had me pay everyone back. Then I closed the business with the IRS and the state, and the remaining money went back into Chester's estate. Violet did, however, give me a nice little bonus for my loyalty to Chester all these years."

A lump formed in Anna's throat. She was afraid this might be the case.

"Was there a lot of money left over?" Anna asked.

"Not as much as you'd think, considering how wealthy Chester had once been. But there was still what most people would consider a sizable amount. Chester left Violet well taken care of. Their house is paid for, and even after the sum that Chester left to his niece, nephews, and brother, she will live comfortably for the rest of her life without having to worry or work."

Anna let out a deep sigh. "I was afraid you would say that."

"What do you mean?" Eliza asked.

"I'm afraid I think I know who killed Chester," Anna replied.

"Please explain it to me, then," Eliza said.

"We know now that Chester had a brain tumor that was affecting his judgement," Anna said. "Until his death, only Violet knew about it."

"That's right," Eliza said. "We all felt badly, because we

blamed him for mistakes that weren't his fault. He was making bad decisions at work and his moods were getting worse, yet Violet was more patient with him than ever. Now we know why."

"Right. Chester continued to make poor business decisions, both with his own money and with that of his friends and family. My guess is that Violet tried to convince him to retire, but he was a stubborn man."

"That's true. He was the very definition of stubborn. If he didn't want to retire, he wouldn't have. Plus, his judgment was poor, anyway. He may not have even realized that he was no longer able to work. But over the past couple of months, he was getting a bad reputation because of his recent failed ventures, so investors were harder to come by. I learned that from talking to some of his associates over the past couple of weeks."

"We know that Violet was devastated that he lost the money of so many good people and that he was on his way to losing his own fortune."

Understanding spread across Todd's face. He leaned back in his chair.

At the same time, Eliza's jaw dropped. "Are you saying that Violet killed Chester to stop him from losing his fortune and from losing any more money from other investors?"

Anna nodded solemnly. "I think that's what happened."

Eliza's hands began to tremble, and her breathing quickened. "No. It can't be." Then Eliza's eyes settled on a spot behind Anna, and her mouth fell open.

Anna and Todd turned and looked behind them. Violet was standing in the doorway.

"Violet," Eliza said. "Please tell me this isn't true."

Tears streamed down Violet's face, but she said nothing.

As Anna, Todd, and Eliza stood up, Violet ran out the door.

"She's early," Eliza said. "She came to take me to lunch on my last day of work."

The three of them chased Violet out the door, down the stairs, into the parking lot, and all the way to Violet's car. With her head start, Violet had made it to her car and was starting her engine before they could catch up with her.

Anna was in the lead. As Violet hit the gas, Anna realized her car was heading straight towards her. She froze.

Seemingly out of nowhere, Todd bolted toward Anna and pushed her out of the way, covering her body with his own.

CHAPTER 28

To her credit, Violet did, at the last moment, attempt to swerve the car to avoid hitting Anna, but if Todd hadn't pushed her out of the way, it may have been too late.

In all the commotion, Violet crashed her car into the chain linked fence that enclosed the parking lot.

Todd stood first and helped Anna up from the ground.

Violet sat in the front seat with her head between her hands, resting it on the steering wheel.

Anna's heart broke for the woman, who in a moment of desperation and misguided concern for her friends and her own future, made a mistake for which she will pay for the rest of her life.

Anna called Charlie, while Eliza went over to comfort her friend.

When Charlie arrived, Violet confessed to everything. It was just as Anna had concluded. Over the past few months, Chester had made a number of bad investments, as Eliza had said. When Violet realized what was happening, she tried to convince Chester to turn over the business to her, but he refused. He insisted that even with a reduced mental capacity, he was still capable of running his business. No matter how much Violet pleaded with him, he refused to let her get involved. In the end, Violet believed she had no other choice but to kill him, so she could protect her own financial future and that of his other heirs.

Anna, Todd, and Eliza went to the police station to give their statements. Eliza had called Allie and Jackson to inform them that Violet had been taken into custody.

Eliza's sons insisted on seeing their mother when she told them what happened, so she went home to meet them. But Anna and Todd went straight to Allie's and Jackson's to see how the couple was doing. Anna imagined they would have a lot of questions.

Ever since Anna figured out who the killer was, her heart had been heavy for Allie.

Nick, Drake, and Oliver were already at the house when they arrived. As Anna suspected, Allie was having a tough time accepting that the killer turned out to be her loving aunt.

"I'm so sorry," Anna said, hugging Allie. "I wish things had turned out differently."

"Why would she have done such a foolish thing?" Allie asked. "What was she thinking?"

"I don't know. But if it's any consolation, in some twisted way, I think she believed she was doing what was best for everyone. Chester was blowing money on bad investments, and she was afraid there would be nothing left for herself and the rest of his heirs. Or to pay back those who had already lost their shirts."

"I was surprised to see a check in the mail from Violet for the amount I lost in Chester's investment," Nick said. "Dorothea told me that she received the same thing, as well as a few other friends. Aunt Violet wouldn't have been able to reimburse us if Chester squandered his fortune on bad investments."

"According to Eliza and Violet, Chester was well on his way to doing just that," Todd said.

"Speaking of Eliza, when she called earlier, she said that Todd saved Anna's life. Was Aunt Violet trying to hurt you?"

Anna shook her head. "No. She overheard us in Chester's office as we put the pieces together and she realized that we knew what she had done. She panicked, ran out of the office, and got into her car. I think she just meant to drive away, and I happened to get in the way. She did swerve her car to try to avoid me, but Todd had already pushed me out of the way." Anna smiled. "By the way, thanks for that, Todd."

He winked at Anna. "We can't have anything happen to Seagull Cove's premier amateur sleuth. Not to mention the owner of my favorite ice cream parlor."

Allie and Jackson looked at each other and smiled. Anna had the feeling they thought that she and Todd were dating, but it didn't seem important enough to correct them.

"As horrible as we feel about the way things turned out, we are so grateful for all you did to help us," Jackson said.

After spending a little while longer with them, Anna and Todd left so the twice-grieving family could be alone. Todd dropped Anna off at her home.

"I have to admit, it was fun solving a murder with you," Todd said.

"I'm not sure if I'd call it *fun*," Anna said with a chuckle. "But we did a good thing together."

Todd smiled. "Now that that's behind us, I'd better get back to work. I didn't intend to be away all day. I'll see you soon at *Bella's Dream*."

"I'll see you soon, Todd."

Anna's stomach reminded her that she had skipped lunch, so she made herself a quick sandwich with a side of potato chips. She looked at the clock on her microwave. It was after 4:00. She had likely missed Joe's daily visit to her shop.

Anna walked toward *Bella's Dream*. When she got close to the shop, she noticed a light on in Joe's second floor apartment. She climbed the stairs and knocked on his door.

Joe looked surprised to see Anna. He stepped back so that she could enter. Anna sat on his sofa, and Joe sat on a well-worn faded green armchair.

"I've been wondering how you are doing. You're not always in the ice cream shop these days when I come in," Joe said. "I figured you must be busy with all your sleuthing."

She wasn't sure which investigation he was referring to, but she assumed he knew that she was involved in Chester's, in addition to Bella's. Nothing got by Joe.

"We just solved Chester's murder," Anna said. "I was working with Todd Devonshire, since he was assisting me at the party when Chester died. Unfortunately, the killer was his wife, Violet. She poisoned him in a misguided attempt to protect herself and her loved ones."

Joe looked toward the ceiling. "There are too many misguided intentions in this world."

"That's what I'm figuring out," Anna said. She thought of her sister. Did Bella stage her death as a misguided attempt to protect her family, or was it necessary under the circumstances?

"You're becoming quite the detective. I used to worry about you, but you've proven you can take care of yourself. Have you ever considered becoming a private investigator?"

That wasn't news to Anna. She had known that she could take care of herself for a long time now. But there was something about hearing Old Joe Wiggins say it that filled her with pride and confidence. A gentle smile found its way to her lips. "Thanks for the compliment, but I have no desire to become a private investigator. I just want to find my sister. The rest of these cases seem to fall on my lap."

"Speaking of Bella, Jeremy said you had some good news about your sister, but that he'd let you tell me."

"Do you know *everything* that happens in Seagull Cove, Joe Wiggins?"

He smirked. "People tend to tell me things."

Joe was right. It was part of his charm. Even Anna couldn't resist telling him things she wouldn't tell anyone else.

"I have some fantastic news. We found a salon in Camden, Maine where Bella worked. It was one of the salons on your list. It's under new ownership, and Bella stopped working there about a year ago, but the new owner remembered her. She's going under the name Izzy, as we thought, and the last she heard, Bella had taken a job as a nail technician at an assisted living facility. We showed the new owner a photo, and she confirmed that it was Bella."

Joe's eyes widened. "That's fantastic, Anna."

"I'm still reeling from the news. Part of me wanted to go straight over to the assisted living facility, but it was late, and she wouldn't have likely been working. If I go and she's not there, I might blow my cover. I was hoping you could help me determine my next step."

Joe leaned back in his armchair and looked past Anna. Then his blue eyes settled on her.

"I agree that you want to maintain the element of surprise. And you need to confront her in a place where she can't run away. I don't want to scare you, Anna, but you may only have one shot at this. If Bella knows you're looking for her, she might run again."

Anna suddenly felt as if a cold hand were squeezing her heart.

"You could call the facility and pretend you would like to tour it for your mother," Joe continued.

"That's a great idea. If Bella is working, I'm sure to see her on the tour. If not, I could casually ask about the services, including nails and hair, and try to ascertain when she works."

"You could pretend that spa services are important to your mother and ask for some details on what they offer and when. If Bella is not working when you go, you can figure out a reason to return for another tour, perhaps say that you'd like another family member to see the facility, as well. Take your time and do this right. You should think about what you will say to her when you see her. She obviously doesn't want to be found, or she would have come out of hiding."

Anna and Joe sat in silence for a few moments. "I think that's the best way to proceed," Anna finally said. "I guess I have some more thinking to do."

"Keep me in the loop. And if you need to talk some more, you know where to find me."

Both excitement and anxiety bounced around in Anna's

stomach like a giant beach ball as she left Joe's apartment to give some more thought to her plan.

She knew she wouldn't be able to think about anything else until she saw Bella with her own eyes.

THE END... **of Book 4**

Anna's adventures in Seagull Cove are far from over! Are you ready to find out what happens next?

Next Book in this Series
Peppermint Stick-Up (Book 5)
Available on Amazon.

* * *

Make sure you're on Angela's mailing list so you can learn about new releases, sales and exclusive content. As a thank you gift for joining Angela's Readers' Group, you will receive a free copy of *Vacations and Victims*, the prequel to the *Sapphire Beach Series.*
Available in ebook and PDF formats at:
BookHip.com/RHFRLNV

STAY IN TOUCH!

Join Angela's Readers' Group so you can learn about new releases, sales, and exclusive content. As a thank you gift, you will receive a free copy of the ebook *Vacations and Victims*, the prequel to the *Sapphire Beach Series*.

To join Angela's Readers' Group, enter your email address at: BookHip.com/RHFRLNV.

Website:
AngelaKRyan.com

Email:
Angela@AngelaKRyan.com

Facebook:
Facebook.com/AngelaKRyanAuthor

Instagram:
Instagram.com/authorangelakryan

Post Office:
Angela K. Ryan, John Paul Publishing,
Post Office Box 283, Tewksbury, MA 01876

ABOUT THE AUTHOR

Angela K. Ryan is the author of the *Seaside Ice Cream Shop Mysteries* and the *Sapphire Beach Cozy Mystery Series*. She writes clean, feel-good cozies for readers who love humor, lots of twists and turns, and happy-dance endings.

When she is not writing, Angela enjoys the outdoors, especially kayaking, stand-up paddleboarding, snowshoeing, and skiing. She lives in Massachusetts and loves all four of the New England seasons, but looks forward to regular escapes to the white, sandy beaches of southwest Florida, where her mother resides.

Angela would happily live in either of the fictitious seaside towns in Massachusetts and Florida where her series take place if it weren't for all the bodies that keep turning up!

Angela dreams of one day owning a Cavalier King Charles Spaniel like the sweet pup in her *Sapphire Beach Series*, but she isn't home enough to take care of one. So, for now, she lives vicariously through one of her main characters, Connie.

Made in the USA
Middletown, DE
10 September 2024